In her blue checked overalls, and with her hair scraped back under a matching scarf, Sarah figured she could easily have passed for a heap of old clothes dumped on the ground were it not for the elaborate trolley of cleaning materials by her side.

She had had dreams once, but that had been five years ago. In a heartbeat all that had changed.

As the hushed voices got closer Sarah put her all into the wretched stain on the carpet, but with a sinking heart she was aware that the voices had fallen silent and the footsteps seemed to have stopped just in front of her.

In fact, sliding her eyes across, she could make out some hand-tailored Italian shoes just below charcoal-grey trousers, sharply creased.

Reluctantly, Sarah raised her eyes, and in that instant she was skewered to the spot by the same bitter chocolate eyes that had taken up residence in her head five years ago and stubbornly refused to budge. Raoul Sinclair.

Cathy Williams is originally from Trinidad, but has lived in England for a number of years. She currently has a house in Warwickshire, which she shares with her husband Richard, her three daughters, Charlotte, Olivia and Emma, and their pet cat, Salem. She adores writing romantic fiction, and would love one of her girls to become a writer—although at the moment she is happy enough if they do their homework and agree not to bicker with one another!

Recent titles by the same author:

THE SECRET SINCLAIR

BY
CATHY WILLIAMS

®recipe and hereaface 11 BY SAAL. The text of this publication may
not thereof may not be reproduced or transmitted in any form
or by any means, electronic or mechanical, including photocopying,
recording, storage in an information retrieval system, or otherwise,
without the written permission of the publisher.

This book is sold subject to the condition that it shall not by way
of trade or otherwise, be lent, resold, hired out or otherwise circulated
without the prior consent of the publisher in any form of binding or
cover other than that in which it is published and without a similar
condition including this condition being imposed on the subsequent
purchaser.

® and TM are trademarks owned and used by the trademark owner
and/or its licensee. Trademarks marked with ® are registered with
the United Kingdom Patent Office and/or the Office for Harmonisation
in the Internal Market and in other countries.

All the characters in this book have no existence outside the imagination
of the author, and have no relation whatsoever to anyone bearing the
same name or names. They are not even distantly inspired by any
individual known or unknown to the author, and all the incidents are
pure invention.

**MORAY COUNCIL
LIBRARIES &
INFO.SERVICES**

20 33 31 74

Askews & Holts

RF

First published in Great Britain 2012
by Mills & Boon, an imprint of Harlequin (UK) Limited.
Harlequin (UK) Limited, Eton House, 18-24 Paradise Road,
Richmond, Surrey TW9 1SR

© Cathy Williams 2012

ISBN: 978 0 263 89033 4

Harlequin (UK) policy is to use papers that are natural, renewable
and recyclable products and made from wood grown in sustainable
forests. The logging and manufacturing process conform to the
legal environmental regulations of the country of origin.

Printed and bound in Spain
by Blackprint CPI, Barcelona

THE SECRET
SINCLAIR

PROLOGUE

RAOUL shifted as quietly as he could on the bed, propped himself up on one elbow and stared down at the woman sleeping contentedly next to him. Through the open window the sultry African night air could barely work itself up into a breeze, and even with the fan lethargically whirring on the chest of drawers it was still and humid. The net draped haphazardly over them was very optimistic protection against the mosquitoes, and as one landed on his arm he slapped it away and sat up.

Sarah stirred, opened her eyes sleepily and smiled at him.

God, he was beautiful. She had never, ever imagined that any man could be as beautiful as Raoul Sinclair. From the very first moment she had laid eyes on him three months ago she had been rendered speechless—and the effect still hadn't worn off.

Amongst all the other people taking their gap years, he stood head and shoulders above the rest. He was literally taller than all of them, but it was much more than that. It was his exotic beauty that held her spellbound: the burnished gold of his skin, the vibrancy of his black, glossy hair—long now; almost to his shoulders—the latent power of his lean, muscular body. Although he was only a matter of a few years older than the rest of them, he was a man amongst boys.

She reached up and skimmed her hand along his back.

'Mosquitoes.' Raoul grinned, dark eyes sweeping over her smooth honey-gold shoulders down to her breasts. He felt himself stirring and hardening, even though they had made love less than a few hours ago. 'This net is useless. But, seeing that we're now both up and wide awake...'

With a little sigh of pleasure Sarah reached out and linked her hands around his neck, drawing him to her and wriggling restlessly as his mouth found hers.

A virgin when she had met him, she knew he had liberated her. Every touch had released new and wonderful sensations.

Her body was slick with heat and perspiration as he gently pulled down the thin sheet which was all they could endure out here.

She had the most wonderful breasts he had ever seen, and with a sudden pang of regret for things to come Raoul realised that he was going to miss her body. No—much more than that. He was going to miss *her*.

It was a situation he had not foreseen when he had decided to take three months off to work in Mozambique. At the time, it had seemed a fitting interlude between the conclusion of university—two hard-won degrees in Economics and Maths—and the start of what he intended to be the rest of his life. Before he threw himself into conquering the world and putting his own personal demons to rest he would immerse himself in the selflessness of helping other people—people as unfortunate as he himself had been, although in a completely different way.

Meeting a woman and falling into bed with her hadn't been on his radar. His libido, like everything else in his life, was just something else he had learnt to control ruthlessly. He had intended to spend three months controlling it.

Sarah Scott, with her tangled blonde hair and her fresh-faced innocence, was certainly not the sort of woman he fancied himself drawn to. He generally went for tougher, more experienced types—women with obvious attractions, who were as willing as he was to have a brief, passionate fling. Women who were ships passing in the night, never dropping anchor and more importantly, never expecting *him* to.

One look at Sarah and he had recognised a girl who would be into anchors being dropped, but it hadn't been enough to keep him away. For two weeks, as they'd been thrown together in circumstances so far removed from reality that it was almost like living in a bubble, he had watched her broodingly out of the corner of his eye, had been aware of her watching him. By the end of week three the inevitable had become reality.

They made love now—quietly and slowly. The house they shared with six other occupants had walls as thin as tracing paper, and wooden floors that seemed to transmit sound with ruthless efficiency.

'Okay,' Raoul whispered, 'how close do you think I can get before you have to stifle a groan?'

'Don't,' Sarah whispered back with a giggle. 'You know how hard it is…'

'Yes, and it's what I like about you. One touch and I can feel your body melt.' He touched her accordingly, a feathery touch between her generous breasts, trailing a continuous line to circle her prominent nipples until she was squirming and breathing quickly, face flushed, her hand curling into his over long hair.

As he delicately licked the stiffened, swollen tip of her nipple he automatically placed a gentle hand over her mouth, and half smiled as she tried very hard not to groan into the palm of his hand.

Only a handful of times had they taken the beaten up Land Rover and escaped to one of the beaches, where they had found privacy and made love without restraint. Between work and down-time on the compound, however, they were confined to a type of lovemaking that was as refined and guarded as a specialised dance.

Sarah half opened her eyes, simply because she could never resist watching Raoul—the dark bronze of his body against the paler gold of hers, the play of sinew and muscle as he reared up over her, powerful and strong and untamed.

Although it was after midnight, the moon was bright and full. Its silvery light streamed through the window, casting shadows on the walls and picking up the hard angles of his face as he licked a path along her stomach, down to where her legs were parted for his eventual caress.

Quite honestly, at times like this Sarah thought that she had died and gone to heaven, and it never failed to amaze her that her feelings for this man could be so overwhelming after only a matter of three months...less! She felt as though, without even realising it, she had been saving herself for him to come along and take possession of her heart.

As their lovemaking gathered urgency the uneasy tangle of thoughts that had been playing in her head for the past few days were lost as he thrust into her and then picked up a long, steady rhythm that became faster and harder, until she felt herself spiralling towards orgasm, holding on so that their bodies became one and they climaxed. The only sounds were their fast-drawn breaths, even though she wanted to cry out loud from the pleasure of fulfilment.

As she tumbled back down to earth the moonlight illuminated his suitcases, packed and standing to attention by the single old-fashioned wardrobe.

And then back came the disquieting thoughts.

Raoul sank against her, spent, and for a few seconds neither of them spoke. He draped his arm over her body. The sheet had managed to work itself into a heap at the foot of the bed, and he idly wondered just how long it would take for the mosquitoes to figure out that there was a new and much bigger entrance available to get inside.

'Can…can we talk?'

Raoul stiffened. Past experience had taught him that anyone who wanted to *talk* invariably wanted to say things he didn't want to hear.

'Okay, I can tell from the way you're not jumping with joy that you don't want to talk, but I think we should. I mean…your cases are all packed, Raoul. You're leaving in two days' time. And I…I don't know what's going to happen to us.'

Raoul swung off her to lie back. He stared at the ceiling in silence for a few seconds. Of course he had known that this was where they would end up, but he had conveniently chosen to ignore that because she had bewitched him. Every time he had considered giving her one of his little speeches about expecting nothing from him he had looked into her bright green eyes and the speech had melted away.

He reluctantly turned to face her and stroked the vanilla blonde hair off her face, neatly tucking loose strands behind her ears.

'I know we need to talk,' he admitted heavily.

'But you still don't want to…'

'I'm not sure where it's going to get us.'

Hearing that was like having ice cold water thrown in her face, but Sarah ploughed on bravely—because she just couldn't see that what they had could possibly come to *nothing* the minute he departed. They had done a thousand things together. More than some people packed into a lifetime. She refused to concede that it could all melt away into nothingness.

'I never intended to come out here and start any kind of relationship,' he confessed, his eloquence for once gone, because he was just not accustomed to having emotional conversations with anyone. He never had. He just didn't think that he had it in him. But there she was, staring at him in the darkness with those big, questioning eyes... waiting.

'Nor did I. I mean, I just wanted to get some experience and live a little—do something a bit different before starting university. You know that. How many times did I tell you that—?' She'd very nearly said *falling in love*, but an innate sense of self-preservation held her back. Not once had he ever told her what he felt for her. She had only deduced from the way he looked at her and touched her, and laughed at the things she said, and when she teased him. 'That meeting someone wasn't part of my agenda either. The unexpected happens.'

Did it? Not to him. Never to him. He had endured a childhood that had been riddled with the unexpected— all of it bad. Top of his list of things to avoid was *The Unexpected*, but she was right. What had blossomed between them had taken him by surprise. He drew her against him and searched for the right words to explain just why the future staring them in the face would be one they each faced on their own.

'I shouldn't have given in, Sarah.'

'Shouldn't have given in to what?'

'You know what. To you.'

'Please don't say that,' she whispered with heartfelt dismay. 'Are you saying that what we did was all a big mistake? We've had so much fun! You don't have to be serious all the time.'

Raoul took her hand and kissed the tips of her fingers, one by one, until the radiant smile reappeared on her face. She smiled easily.

'It's been fun,' he agreed, with the heavy feeling of someone about to deliver a fatal blow to an unsuspecting victim. 'But this isn't reality, Sarah. This is time out. You pretty much said it yourself. Reality is what's in front of us. In your case three years at university. In my case...' *The world and nothing less.* 'A job. I really hoped that we wouldn't have to have this conversation. I hoped that you would see what's pretty clear to me. This has been great, but it's...a holiday affair.'

'A holiday affair?' Sarah repeated in a small voice.

Raoul sighed and ran his fingers through his too-long hair. He would get rid of it the second he made it back to civilisation.

'Don't make me out to be an ogre, Sarah. I'm not saying that it hasn't been...incredible. It has. In fact, it's been the most incredible three months of my life.' He hesitated. His past had never been something he chose to discuss with anyone, least of all a woman, but the urge to go further with her was overpowering. 'You've made me feel like no one else ever has...but then I suppose you know that...'

'How can I when you've never told me?' But it was something for her to hang onto.

'I...I'm not good with this kind of emotional drama. I've had a lot of emotional drama in my life...'

'What do you mean?' She knew only the barest of facts about his past, even though he pretty much knew everything about hers. She had waxed lyrical about her childhood—her very happy and very ordinary childhood—as an only child of two parents who had always thought that they would never have kids until her mother became pregnant at the merry age of forty-one.

He had skirted round the subject aside from telling her that he'd had no parents, preferring to concentrate on the future which, as time went on, suited her very well—even though any mention of *her* in that future hadn't actually been voiced. She liked the thought of him forging his way with her at his side. Somewhere.

'I grew up in a foster home, Sarah. I was one of those kids you read about in the newspapers who get taken in by Social Services because their parents can't take care of them.'

Sarah sat up, lost for words. Then her natural warmth took over and she felt the prickle of tears, which brought a reluctant smile to his lips.

'Neither of your parents could look after you?'

'Just the one parent on the scene. My mother.' It was not in his nature to confide, and he picked carefully at his words, choosing to denude them of all potency. It was a trick he had learnt a long time ago, so his voice, when he spoke, was flat and detached. 'Unfortunately she had a problem with substances, which ended up killing her when I was five. My father... Who knows? Could have been anyone.'

'You poor soul!'

'I prefer to think of my background as character-building, and as foster homes went mine wasn't too bad. Where I'm going with this...' For a second he had to remind himself where he *was* going with it. 'I'm not looking for a relationship. Not now—probably not ever. I never meant to string you along, Sarah, but...you got under my skin... And all *this* didn't exactly go the distance in bringing me back to my senses.'

'All what?'

'Here. The middle of nowhere. Thrown together in the heat…'

'So nothing would have happened between us if we hadn't been out here?' She could hear her voice rising and had to control it, because she didn't want to wake anyone—although there was only one other English speaking person on the compound.

'That's a purely hypothetical question.'

'You could try answering it!'

'I don't know.' He could feel the hurt seeping out of her, but what could he do about it? How could he make it better without issuing promises he knew he wouldn't keep?

Frustration and anger at himself rushed through him in a tidal wave. Hell, he should have known just by looking at her that Sarah wasn't one of those women who were out to have a good time, no strings attached! Where had his prized self-control been when he had needed it most? Absent without leave! He had seen her and all trace of common sense had deserted him.

And when he had discovered that she was a virgin? Had that stopped him in his tracks? The opposite. He had felt unaccountably thrilled to be her first, had wanted to shout it from the rooftops. Instead of backing away he had rushed headlong into the sort of crazy quasi-romantic situation that he had always scorned. There hadn't been chocolates and jewellery—not that he could have afforded either—but there had been long, lazy conversations, a great deal of laughter… Hell, he had even cooked her a meal on one occasion, when the rest of the crew had disappeared for the weekend to camp on the beach, leaving the two of them in charge.

'You don't know? Is that because I'm not really your type?'

He hesitated just long enough for her to bitterly assume the obvious.

'I'm not, am I?' She slung her legs over the bed, kicking away at the mosquito net and finally shoving it aside so that she could crawl under it.

'Where are you going!'

'I don't want to be having this conversation.' In the darkness she hunted around for her clothes, located them, and began putting them on. An old tee shirt, a pair of denim shorts, her flipflops. 'I'm going outside. I need to get some air.'

Raoul debated the wisdom of following her for a few seconds, then leapt out of the bed, struggling with his jeans, not bothering with a shirt at all, as he watched her flying out of the room like a bat out of hell.

The bedroom was small, equipped with the most basic of furniture, and cluttered with all the bits and pieces of two occupants. He came close to tripping over one of his shoes and cursed softly under his breath. He shouldn't be following her. He had said all there was to say on the subject of any continuing romance. To prolong the conversation would be to invite a debate that would be stillborn, so what was the point? But watching her disappear through the bedroom door had galvanised him into instant, inexplicable action.

The house was a square concrete block, its front door accessed by sufficient steps to ensure that it was protected against flooding during the cyclone season.

He caught up with her just as she had reached the bottom of the steps.

'So, what *are* your types!' Sarah swung round to glare at him, hands on her hips.

'Types? What are you talking about?'

'These women you go for?'

'That's irrelevant.'

'Not to me it isn't!' Sarah stared up at him. She was shaking like a leaf, and she didn't know why she was getting hung up on that one detail. He was right. It was irrelevant. What did it matter if he went for tall brunettes and she was a short blonde? What mattered was that he was dumping her. Throwing her out like used goods. Tossing her aside as though she was just something insignificant that no longer mattered. When he was *everything* to her.

She literally shied away from the thought of waking up in three days' time in an empty bed, knowing that she would never lay eyes on him again. How on earth was she going to survive?

'You need to calm down.' He shook his head and raked his fingers through his hair, sweeping it back from his face. God, it was like an oven out here. He could feel the sweat beginning to gather on his body.

'I'm perfectly calm!' Sarah informed him in a shrill voice. 'I just want to know if you've had fun *using* me for the past three months!'

She swung round, began heading towards the central clearing, where the circular reed huts with their distinctive pointed roofs were used as classrooms for the twenty local children who attended every day. Raoul didn't teach. He and two of the other guys did brutally manual labour—building work in one of the communities further along, planting and harvesting of crops. He gave loads of advice on crop rotation and weather patterns. He seemed to know absolutely everything.

'Were you just making the best of a bad job out here? Sleeping with me because there was no one else around to your taste?'

'Don't be stupid!' He reached out and stopped her in her tracks, pulling her back to him and forcing her to look up.

'I know I'm not the most glamorous person in the world. I know you're probably accustomed to landing really gorgeous girls.' She bit her lip and looked away, feeling miserable and thoroughly sorry for herself. 'I knew it was odd that you even looked at me in the first place, but I suppose I was the only other English person here so you made do.'

'Don't do this, Sarah,' Raoul said harshly. He could feel her trembling against him, and he had to fight the impulse to terminate the conversation by kissing that lush, full mouth. 'If you want to know what kind of women I've always gone for, I'll tell you. I've always gone for women who wanted nothing from me. I'm not saying that's a good thing, but it's the truth. Yes, they've been good looking, but not in the way that you are…'

'What way is that?' Sarah asked scornfully, but she was keen to grasp any positive comment in these suddenly turbulent waters. She realised with a sinking heart that she would be willing to beg for him. It went against every grain of pride in her, but, yes, she would plead for him at least to keep in touch.

'Young, innocent, full of laughter…' He loosened his fingers on her arm and gently stroked her. 'That's why I should have run a mile the minute you looked at me with those big green eyes,' he murmured with genuine regret. 'But I couldn't. You summed up everything I wasn't looking for, and I still couldn't resist you.'

'You don't have to!' Before he could knock her last-ditch plea down in flames she turned away brusquely and walked towards the clearing, adopting a position on one of the fallen tree trunks which had been left as a bench of sorts.

Her heart was beating like a jackhammer and she could barely catch her breath. She didn't look at him as he sat down on the upturned trunk next to her.

The night was alive with the sounds of insects and frogs, but it was cooler out here than it had been in the stifling heat of the bedroom.

Eventually she turned to him. 'I'm not asking you to settle down and marry me,' she said quietly—although, really, who was she kidding? That was exactly what she wanted. 'But you don't have to walk away and never look back. I mean, we can keep in touch.' She threw him a watery, desperate smile. 'That's what mobile phones and e-mails and all these social networking sites are all about, you know.'

'How many times have we argued about the merits of throwing your personal life into a public arena for the world to feed on?'

'You're such a dinosaur, Raoul.' But she smiled. They'd argued about so many things! Light-hearted arguments, with lots of laughter. When Raoul took a stand it was impossible to deflect him, and she had enjoyed teasing him about his implacability. She had never known anything like it.

'And you'd be happy to do that?' Raoul thought that if she were the kind of girl who could be happy with that kind of distant, intermittent contact then they wouldn't be sitting here right now, having this conversation, because then she would also be the kind of girl who would have indulged in a three-month fling and been happy to walk away, without agonising about a future that wasn't destined to be.

For a fleeting moment he wondered what it would be like to take her with him, but the thought was one he discarded even before it had had time to take root. He was a product of his background, and that was something he was honest enough to acknowledge.

Deprived of stability, he had learnt from a very young

age that he had to look out for himself. He couldn't even really remember when he had made his mind up that the world would never decide his fate. He would control it, and the way he would do that would be through his brains. Foster care had honed his single-minded ambition and provided him with one very important lesson in life: rely on no one.

Whilst the other kids had been larking around, or pining for parents that failed to show up at appointed times, he had buried his head in books and mastered all the tricks of studying in the midst of chaos. Blessed with phenomenal intelligence, he had sailed through every exam, and as soon as he'd been released from the restrictions of a foster home had worked furiously to put himself through college and then later university.

Starting with nothing, he had to do more than just *be clever*. A degree counted for nothing when you were competing with someone who had family connections. So he had got two degrees—two high-powered degrees—which he intended to use ruthlessly to get where he wanted to go.

Where, in his great scheme of things, would Sarah fit in? He was no carer and never would be. He just didn't have it in him. And Sarah was the sort of soft, gentle person who would always need someone to take care of her.

Heck, she couldn't even bring herself to answer his question! When she spoke of keeping in touch, what she really meant was having an ongoing relationship. How responsible would he be if he told her what she wanted to hear?

Abruptly Raoul stood up, putting some vital immediate distance between them—because sitting next to her was doing crazy things to his thoughts and to his body.

'Well?' he asked, more harshly than he had intended, and he sensed her flinch as she bowed her head. He had to use every scrap of will-power at his disposal not to go across and put his arms around her. He clenched his hands into fists, wanting to hit something very hard. 'You haven't answered my question. *Could* you keep in touch with me with the occasional e-mail? When you should be moving on? Putting me behind you and chalking the whole thing up to experience?'

'How can you be so callous?' Sarah whispered. She had practically begged and it hadn't been enough. He didn't love her and he never would. Why should she waste her time lamenting the situation? He was right. E-mails and text messages would just prolong the hurt. She needed to cut him out of her life and leave no remaining bits to fester and multiply.

'I'm not being callous, Sarah. I'm sparing you the pain of building false hopes. You're young, with stars in your eyes...'

'You're not exactly over the hill, Raoul!'

'In terms of experience I'm a thousand years older than you, and I'm not the man you're looking for. I would be no good for you...'

'That's usually the coward's way out of a sticky situation,' she muttered, having read it somewhere and thought that it made sense.

'In this case it's the truth. You need someone who's going to take care of you, and that person is never going to be me.' He watched her carefully and wondered if he would ever again be in the business of justifying himself to another human being. *Walk alone,* that was what he had taught himself, *and you don't end up entangled in situations such as this.* 'I don't want the things that you do,' he continued softly.

Sarah would have liked to deny that she wanted any of those things he accused her of wanting, but she did. She wanted the whole fairytale romance and he knew it. It felt as if he knew her better than anyone ever had.

Her shoulders slumped as she struggled to look for the silver lining in the cloud. There always was one.

'I'm not equipped for playing happy families, Sarah…'

She eventually raised her eyes to his and looked at him coldly. 'You're right. I want all that stuff, and it *is* better for you to let me down so that I can have a fighting chance of meeting someone who isn't scared of commitment.' Her legs felt like jelly when she stood up. 'It would be awful to think that I might waste my time loving you when you haven't *got it in you* for the fairytale stuff!'

Raoul gritted his teeth, but there was nothing to say in response to that.

'And by the way,' she flung over her shoulder, 'I'll leave your clothes outside the bedroom door, because I'll be sleeping on my own tonight! You want your precious freedom so badly? Well, congratulations—you've got it!'

She kept her head held high as she covered the ten thousand miles back to the house. At least it felt like ten thousand miles.

Memories of their intense relationship flashed through her head like a slow, painful slideshow. Thinking about him could still give her goosebumps, and she hugged herself as she jogged up the flight of stone steps to the front door.

In the bedroom, she gathered up some of his clothes and buried her face in them, breathing in his musky, aggressively male scent, then duly stuck them outside—along with his cases.

Then she locked the bedroom door, and in the empty quiet of the bedroom contemplated a life without Raoul in it and tried to stop the bottom of her world from dropping out.

CHAPTER ONE

CAUGHT in the middle of crouching on the ground, trying to get rid of a particularly stubborn stain on the immaculate cream carpet that ran the length, breadth and width of the directors' floor of the very exclusive family bank in which she had now been working for the past three weeks, Sarah froze at the sound of voices emerging from one of the offices. Low, unhurried voices—one belonging to a man, the other to a woman.

It was the first time she had been made aware of any sign of life here. She came at a little after nine at night, did her cleaning and left. She liked it that way. She had no wish to bump into anyone—not that there would have been the slightest possibility of her being addressed. She was a cleaner, and as such was rendered instantly invisible. Even the doorman who had been allowing her entry ever since she had started working at the bank barely glanced up when she appeared in front of him.

She could barely remember a time when she had been able to garner a few admiring glances. The combined weight of responsibility and lack of money had rubbed the youthful glow from her face. Now when she looked in the mirror all she saw was a woman in her mid-twenties with shadows under her eyes and the pinched appearance of someone with too many worries.

Sarah wondered what she should do. Was there some special etiquette involved if a cleaner come into contact with one of the directors of this place? She hunkered down. In her blue checked overalls and with her hair scraped back under a matching scarf, she figured she might easily have passed for a heap of old clothes dumped on the ground, were it not for the elaborate trolley of cleaning materials by her side.

As the hushed voices got closer—just round the corner—Sarah put her all into the wretched stain on the carpet. But with a sinking heart she was aware that the voices had fallen silent, and the footsteps seemed to have stopped just in front of her.

In fact, sliding her eyes across, she could make out some hand-made Italian shoes just below charcoal-grey trousers, sharply creased, a pair of very high cream stilettos, and stockings with a slight sheen, very sheer.

'I don't know if you've done the conference room as yet, but if you have then you've made a very poor job of it. There are ring marks on the table, and two champagne glasses are still there on the bookshelf!'

The woman's voice was icy cold and imperious. Reluctantly Sarah raised her eyes, travelling the length of a very tall, very thin, very blonde woman in her thirties. From behind her she could hear the man pressing for the lift.

'I haven't got to the conference room yet,' Sarah mumbled. She prayed that the woman wouldn't see fit to lodge a complaint. She needed this job. The hours suited her, and it was well paid for what it was. Included in the package was the cost of a taxi to and from her house to the bank. How many cleaning jobs would ever have included *that*?

'Well, I'm relieved to hear it!'

'For God's sake, Louisa, let the woman do her job. It's

nearly ten, and I can do without spending the rest of the evening here!'

Sarah heard that voice—the voice that had haunted her for the past five years—and her mind went a complete blank. Then it was immediately kick-started, papering over the similarities of tone. Because there was no way that Raoul Sinclair could be the man behind her. Raoul Sinclair was just a horrible, youthful mistake that was now in the past.

And yet…

Obeying some kind of primitive instinct to match a face to that remarkable voice, Sarah turned around—and in that instant she was skewered to the spot by the same bitter chocolate eyes that had taken up residence in her head five years ago and stubbornly refused to budge. She half stood, swayed.

The last thing she heard before she fainted was the woman saying, in a shrill, ringing voice, 'Oh, for God's sake, that's the *last thing we need*!'

She came to slowly. As her eyelids fluttered open she knew, in a fuddled way, that she really didn't want to wake up. She wanted to stay in her peaceful faint.

She had been carried into an office and was now on a long, low sofa which she recognised as the one in Mr Verrier's office. She tried to struggle upright and Raoul came into her line of vision, taller than she remembered, but just as breathtakingly beautiful. She had never seen him in anything dressier than a pair of jeans and an old tee shirt, and she was slowly trying to match up the Raoul she had known with this man kneeling over her, who looked every inch the billionaire he had once laughingly informed her he would be.

'Here—drink this.'

'I don't want to drink anything. What are you doing here? Am I seeing things? You can't be here.'

'Funny, but I was thinking the very same thing.' Raoul had only now recovered his equilibrium. The second his eyes had locked onto hers he had been plunged into instant flashback, and carrying her into the office had reawakened a tide of feeling which he had assumed to have been completely exorcised. He remembered the smell of her and the feel of her as though it had been yesterday. How was that possible? When so much had happened in the intervening years?

Sarah was fighting to steady herself. She couldn't believe her eyes. It was just so weird that she had to bite back the desire to burst into hysterical, incredulous laughter.

'What are you doing here, Sarah? Hell...you've changed...'

'I know.' She was suddenly conscious of the sight she must make, scrawny and hollow-cheeked and wearing her overalls. 'I have, haven't I?' She nervously fingered the checked overall and knew that she was shaking. 'Things haven't worked out...quite as I'd planned.' She made a feeble attempt to stand up, and collapsed back down onto the sofa.

In truth, Raoul was horrified at what he saw. Where was the bright-eyed, laughing girl he had known?

'I have to go... I have to finish the cleaning, Raoul. I...'

'You're not finishing anything. Not just at the moment. When was the last time you ate anything? You look as though you could be blown away by a gust of wind. And *cleaning*? Now you're doing cleaning jobs to earn money?'

He vaulted to his feet and began pacing the floor. He could scarcely credit that she was lying on the sofa in this office. Accustomed to eliminating any unwelcome emotions and reactions as being surplus to his finely tuned and highly controlled way of life, he found that he couldn't control the bombardment of questions racing through his brain. Nor could he rein in the flood of unwanted memories that continued to besiege him from every angle.

Sarah was possibly the very last woman with whom he had had a perfectly natural relationship. She represented a vision of himself as a free man, with one foot on the ladder but no steps actually yet taken. Was that why the impact of seeing her again now was so powerful?

'I never meant to end up like this,' Sarah whispered, as the full impact of their unexpected meeting began to take shape.

'But you have. How? What happened to you? Did you decide that you preferred cleaning floors to teaching?'

'Of course I didn't!' Sarah burst out sharply. She dragged herself into an upright position on the sofa and was confronted with the unflattering sight of her sturdy work shoes and thick, black woollen tights.

'Did you ever make it to university?' Raoul demanded. As she had struggled to sit up his eyes had moved of their own volition to the swing of her breasts under the hideous checked overall.

'I…I left the compound two weeks after you left.'

Her strained green eyes made her look so young and vulnerable that sudden guilt penetrated the armour of his formidable self control.

In five years Raoul had fulfilled every promise he had made to himself as a boy. Equipped with his impressive qualifications, he had landed his first job on the trading floor at the Stock Exchange, where his genius for making money had very quickly catapulted him upwards. Where colleagues had conferred, he'd operated solely on his own, and in the jungle arena of the money-making markets it hadn't been long before he'd emerged as having a killer streak that could make grown men quake in their shoes.

Raoul barely noticed. Money, for him, equated with freedom. He would be reliant on no one. Within three years he had accumulated sufficient wealth to begin the process of acquisition, and every acquisition had been bigger and more impressive than the one before. Guilt had played no part in his meteoric upward climb, and he had had no use for it.

Now, however, he felt it sink its teeth in, and he shoved his fingers through his hair.

Sarah followed the gesture which was so typically him. 'You've had your hair cut,' she said, flushing at the inanity of her observation, and Raoul offered her a crooked half-smile.

'I discovered that shoulder-length hair didn't go with the image. Now, of course, I could grow it down to my waist and no one would dare say a word, but my days of long hair are well and truly over.'

Just as she was, she thought. She belonged to those days that were well and truly over—except they weren't, were they? She knew that there were things that needed to be said, but it was a conversation she'd never expected to have, and now that it was staring her in the face she just wanted to delay its onset for as long as possible.

'You must be pleased.' Sarah stared down at her feet and sensed him walk towards her until his shadow joined her feet. When he sat down next to her, her whole body stiffened in alarm—because even through the nightmare of her situation, and the pain and misery of how their relationship had ended, her body was still stirring into life and reacting to his proximity. 'You were always so determined...' she continued.

'In this life it's the only way to go forward. You were telling me what happened to your university career...'

'Was I?' She glanced across at him and licked her lips nervously. For two years she had done nothing but think of him. Over time the memories had faded, and she had learnt the knack of pushing them away whenever they threatened to surface, but there had been moments when she had flirted with the notion of meeting him again, had created conversations in her head in which she was strong and confident and in control of the situation. Nothing like this.

'I...I never made it to university. Like I said, things didn't quite work out.'

'Because of me.' Raoul loathed this drag on his emotions. Nor could he sit so close to her. Frustrated at the way his self-control had slipped out of his grasp, he pulled a chair over and positioned it directly in front of the sofa. 'You weren't due to leave that compound for another three months. In fact, I remember you saying that you thought you would stay there for much longer.'

'Not all of us make plans that end up going our way,' she told him, with creeping resentment in her voice.

'And you blame me for the fact that you've ended up where you have? I was honest with you. I believe your parting shot was that you were grateful that you would have the opportunity to find Mr Right... If you're going to try and pin the blame for how your life turned out on me, then it won't work. We had a clean break, and that's always the best way. If the Mr Right you found turned out to be the sort of guy who sits around while his woman goes out cleaning to earn money, then that's a pity—but not my fault.'

'This is crazy. I...I'm not blaming you for anything. And there's no *Mr Right*. Gosh, Raoul...I can't believe this. It feels like some kind of…of…nightmare… I don't mean that. I just mean…you're so *different*…'

Raoul chose to ignore her choice of words. She was in a state of shock. So was he. 'Okay, so maybe you didn't find the man of your dreams…but there must have been someone…' he mused slowly. 'Why else would you have abandoned a career you were so passionate about? Hell, you used to say that you were born to teach.'

Sarah raised moss-green eyes to his and he felt himself tense at the raw memory of how she'd used to look up at him, teasing and adoring at the same time. He had revelled in it. Now he doubted that any woman would have the temerity to tease him. Wealth and power had elevated him to a different place—a place where women batted their eyelashes, and flattered…but *teased*? No. Nor would he welcome it. In five years he had not once felt the slightest temptation to dip his toes into the murky waters of commitment.

'Did you get involved with some kind of loser?' he grated. She had been soft and vulnerable and broken-hearted. Had someone come along and taken advantage of her state of mind?

'What are you talking about?'

'You must have been distraught to have returned from Africa ahead of schedule. I realise that you probably blame me for that, but if you had stuck it out you would forgotten me within a few weeks.'

'Is that how it worked for you, Raoul?'

Pinned to the spot by such a direct question, Raoul refused to answer. 'Did you get strung along by someone who promised you the earth and then did a runner when he got tired of you? Is that what happened? A degree would have been your passport, Sarah. How many times did we have conversations about this? What did he say to you to convince you that it was a good idea to dump your aspirations?'

He didn't know whether to stand or to sit. He felt peculiarly uncomfortable in his own skin, and those wide green eyes weren't helping matters.

'And why cleaning? Why not an office job somewhere?'

He looked down at his watch and realised that it was nearing midnight, but he was reluctant to end the conversation even though he queried where it was going. She was just another part of his history, a jigsaw puzzle piece that had already been slotted in place, so why prolong the catch-up game? Especially when those huge, veiled, accusing green eyes were reminding him of a past for which he had no use?

If he politely ushered her to the door he was certain that she would leave and not look back. Which was clearly a good thing.

'You can't trust people,' he advised her roughly. 'Now perhaps you'll see my point of view when I told you that the only person you can rely on is yourself.'

'I've probably lost my job here,' Sarah intoned distractedly.

She had seen him look at his watch and she knew what that meant. Her time was coming to an end. He had moved onwards and upwards to that place where time was money. Reminiscing, for Raoul, would have very limited interest value. He was all about the future, not the past. But she had to plough on and get where she needed to get, horrible though the prospect was.

'I couldn't countenance you working here anyway,' Raoul concurred smoothly.

'What does this place have to do with you?'

'As of six this evening—everything. I own it.'

Sarah's mouth dropped open. 'You own *this*?'

'All part of my portfolio.'

It seemed to Sarah now that there was no meeting point left between them. He had truly moved into a different stratosphere. He literally owned the company whose floors she had been scrubbing less than two hours ago. In his smart business suit, with the silk tie and the gleaming hand-made shoes, he was the absolute antithesis of her, with her company uniform and her well-worn flats.

Defiantly she pulled off the headscarf—if only to diminish the image of complete servility.

Hair the colour of vanilla, soft and fine and unruly, tumbled out. He had cut his hair. She had grown hers. It tumbled nearly to her waist, and for a few seconds Raoul was dazzled at the sight of it.

She was twisting the unsightly headscarf between her fingers, and that brought him back down to earth. She had been saying something about the job—this glorious cleaning job—which she would have to abandon. Unless, of course, she carried on cleaning way past her finishing time.

He'd opened his mouth to continue their conversation, even though he had been annoyingly thrown off course by that gesture of hers, when she said, in such a low voice that he had to strain forward to hear her, 'I tried to get in touch, you know...'

'I beg your pardon?'

Sarah cleared her throat. 'I tried to get in touch, but I...I couldn't...'

Raoul stiffened. Having money had been a tremendous learning curve. It had a magnetism all of its own. People he had once known and heartily wished to forget had made contact, having glimpsed some picture of him in the financial pages of a newspaper. It would have been amusing had it not been so pathetic.

He tried to decipher what Sarah was saying now. Had she been one of those people as well? Had she turned to the financial news and spotted him, thought that she might get in touch as she was down on her luck?

'What do you mean, *you couldn't*?' His voice was several shades cooler.

'I had no idea how to locate you.' Her heart was beating so hard that she felt positively sick. 'I mean, you disappeared without a trace. I tried checking with the girl who kept all the registration forms for when we were out there, and she gave me an address, but you'd left...'

'When did all this frantic checking take place?'

'When I got back to England. I know you dumped me, Raoul, but...but I had to talk to you...'

So despite all her bravado when they had parted company she had still tried to track him down. It was a measure of her lack of sophistication that she had done that, and an even greater measure of it that she would now openly confess to doing so.

'I came to London and rented a room in a house out east. You would never have found me.'

'I even went on the internet, but you weren't to be found. And of course I remembered you saying that you would never join any social networking sites...'

'Quite a search. What was that in aid of? A general chat?'

'Not exactly.'

Sarah was thinking now that if she had carried on searching just a little bit longer—another year or so— then she would have found him listed somewhere on the computer, because he would have made his fortune by then. But she had quickly given up. She had never imagined that he would have risen so far, so fast, and yet when she thought about it there had always been that stubborn, closed, ruthless streak to him. And he had been fearless. Fearless when it came to the physical stuff and fearless when it came to plans for his future.

'I wish I had managed to get through to you. You never kept in touch with your last foster home, did you? I tried to trace you through them, but you had already dropped off their radar.'

Raoul stilled, because he had forgotten just how much she knew about him—including his miserable childhood and adolescence.

'So you didn't get in touch,' he said, with a chill in his voice. 'We could carry on discussing all the various ways you tried and failed to find me, or we could just move on. *Why* did you want to get in touch?'

'You mean that I should have had more pride than to try?'

'A lot of women would have,' Raoul commented drily. She turned her head and the overhead light caught her hair, turning it into streaks of gold and pale toffee. 'But I suppose you were very young. Just nineteen.'

'And too stupid to do the sensible thing?'

'Just...very young.' He dragged his eyes away from the dancing highlights of her hair and frowned, sensing an edginess to her voice although her face was very calm and composed.

'You can't blame me if I couldn't find you...'

Raoul was confused. What was she talking about?

'It's getting late, Sarah. I've worked through the night, hammering out this deal with lawyers. I haven't got the time or the energy to try and decipher what you're saying. Why would I *blame* you for not being able to find me?'

'I'll get to the point. I didn't *want* to get in touch with you, Raoul. What kind of a complete loser do you imagine I am? Do you think that I would have come crawling to you for a second chance?'

'You might have if you'd been through the mill with some other guy!'

'There *was* no other guy! And why on earth would I come running to *you* when you had already told me that you wanted nothing more to do with me?'

'Then why *did* you try and get in touch?' He felt disproportionately pleased that there had been no other guy, but he immediately put that down to the fact that, whether they had parted on good terms or not, he wouldn't have wanted her to be used and tossed aside by someone she had met on the rebound.

'Because I found out that I was pregnant!'

The silence that greeted this pooled around her until Sarah began to feel dizzy.

Raoul was having trouble believing what he had just heard. In fact he was tempted to dismiss it as a trick of the imagination, or else some crazy joke—maybe an attention-seeking device to prolong their conversation.

But one look at her face told him that this was no joke.

'That's the most ridiculous thing I've ever heard, and you have to be nuts if you think I'm going to fall for it. When it comes to money, I've heard it all.' Like a caged beast, he shot up and began prowling through the room, hands shoved into his pockets. 'So we've met again by chance. You're down on your luck, for whatever reason, and you see that I've made my fortune. Just come right out and ask for a helping hand! Do you think I'd turn you away? If you need cash, I can write a cheque for you right now.'

'Stop it, Raoul. I'm not a gold-digger! Just listen to me! I tried to get in touch with you because I found out that I was having your baby. I knew you'd be shocked and, believe me, I did think it over for a while, but in the end I thought that it was only fair that you knew. How could you think that I'd make something like that up to try and get money out of you? Have you ever known me to be materialistic? How could you be so insulting?'

'I couldn't have got you pregnant. It's not possible! I was always careful.'

'Not always,' Sarah muttered.

'Okay, so maybe you got yourself pregnant by someone else…'

'There *was* no one else! When I left the compound I had no idea that I was pregnant. I left because…because I just couldn't stay there any longer. I got back to England and I still intended to start university. I *wanted* to put you behind me. I didn't find out until I was nearly five months along. My periods were erratic, and then they disappeared, but I was so… I barely noticed…'

She had been so miserable that World War III could have broken out and she probably wouldn't have noticed the mushroom cloud outside her bedroom window. Memories of him had filled every second of every minute of her every waking hour, until she had prayed for amnesia—anything that would help her forget. Her parents had been worried sick. At any rate, her mother had been the first to suspect something when she'd begun to look a little rounder, despite the fact that her eating habits had taken a nosedive.

'I'm not hearing this.'

'You don't *want* to hear this! My mum and dad were very supportive. They never once lectured, and they were there for me from the very minute that Oliver was born.'

Somehow the mention of a name made Raoul blanch. It was much harder to dismiss what she had said as the rantings of an ex-lover who wanted money from him and was prepared to try anything to get it. The mention of a name seemed to turn the fiction she was spinning into something approaching reality, and yet still his mind refused to concede that the story being told had anything to do with him.

He'd never been one to shy away from the truth, however brutal, but the nuts and bolts of his sharp brain now seemed to be malfunctioning.

Sarah wished he would say something. Did he really believe that she was making up the whole thing? How suspicious of other people had he become over the years? The young man she had fallen in love with had been fiercely independent—but to this extent? How valuable was his wealth if he now found himself unable to trust anyone around him?

'I…I lived in Devon with them after Oliver was born,' she continued into the deafening silence. 'It wasn't ideal, but I really needed the support. Then about a year ago I decided to move to London. Oliver was older—nearly at school age. I thought I could put him into a nursery part-time. There were no real jobs to be had in our village in Devon, and I didn't want to put Mum and Dad in a position of being permanent babysitters. Dad retired a couple of years ago, and they had always planned to travel. I thought that I would be able to get something here—maybe start thinking about getting back into education…'

'Getting back into education? Of course. It's never too late.' He preferred to dwell on this practical aspect to their conversation, but there was a growing dread inside him. There had been more than one occasion when he had not taken precautions. Somehow it had been a different world out there—a world that hadn't revolved around the usual rules and regulations.

'But it was all harder than I thought it was going to

be.' Sarah miserably babbled on to cover her unease. He thought she had lied to try and get money out of him. There was not even a scrap of affection left for her if he could think that. 'I found a house to rent. It's just a block away from a friend I used to go to school with. Emily. She babysits Oliver when I do jobs like these...'

'You mean you've done nothing but mop floors and clean toilets since you moved here?'

'I've earned a living!' Sarah flared back angrily. 'Office jobs are in demand, and it's tough when you haven't got qualifications or any sort of work experience. I've also done some waitressing and bar work, and in a month's time I'm due to start work as a teaching assistant at the local school. Aren't you going to ask me any questions about your son? I have a picture... In my bag downstairs...'

Raoul was slowly beginning to think the unimaginable, but he was determined to demonstrate that he was no push-over—even for her. Even for a woman who still had the ability to creep into his head when he was least expecting it.

'I grant that you may well have had a child,' he said heavily. 'It's been five years. Anything could have happened during that time. But if you insist on sticking to this story, then I have to tell you that I will want definite proof that the child is mine.'

Every time the word *child* crossed his lips, the fact of it being his seemed to take on a more definite shape. After his uncertain and unhappy past, he had always been grimly assured of one thing: no children. He had seen first-hand the lives that could be wrecked by careless parenting. He had been the victim of a woman who had had a child only to discover that it was a hindrance she could have well done without. Fatherhood was never going to be for him. Now, the possibility of it being dropped on him from a very great height was like being hit by a freight train at full speed.

'I think you'll agree that that's fair enough, given the circumstances,' he continued as he looked at her closed, shocked face.

'You just need to take one look at him... I can tell you his birth date...and you can do the maths...'

'Nothing less than a full DNA test will do.'

Sarah swallowed hard. She tried to see things from his point of view. An accidental meeting with a woman he'd thought left behind for good, and, hey presto, he discovered that he was a father! He would be reeling from shock. Of course he would want to ensure that the child was his before he committed himself to anything! He was now the leading man in his very own worst nightmare scenario. He would want proof!

But the hurt, pain and anger raged through her even as she endeavoured to be reasonable.

He might not want her around. In fact he might, right now, be sincerely hoping that he would wake up and discover that their encounter had been a bad dream. But didn't he know her at all? Didn't he *know* that she was not the type of girl who would ever *lie* to try and wrangle money out of him?

Unhappily, she was forced to concede that time had changed them both.

Whilst she had been left with her dreams in tatters around her, a single mother scraping to make ends meet and trying to work out how she could progress her career in the years to come, he had forgotten her and moved on. He had realised his burning ambitions and was now in a place from which he could look down at her like a Greek god, contemplating a mere mortal.

She shuddered to think what would have happened had she managed to locate him all those years ago.

'Of course,' she agreed, standing up.

She could feel a headache coming on. In the morning, Oliver would be at playgroup. She would try and catch up on some sleep while the house was empty. It hadn't escaped her notice that Raoul still hadn't shown any appetite for finding out what his son was like.

'I should go.'

In the corner of her eye, the cleaning trolley was a forlorn reminder of how her life had abruptly changed in the space of a few hours and suddenly become much more complicated. She doggedly reminded herself that whatever the situation *between them* it was good that he knew about Oliver. She sneaked a glance at him from under her lashes and found him staring down at her with an unreadable expression.

'I'm very sorry about this, Raoul.' She dithered, awkward and self-conscious in her uniform. 'I know the last thing you probably want is to have bumped into me and been told that you've fathered a child. Believe me, I don't expect you to do anything. You can walk away from the situation. It's only going to clutter up your life.'

Raoul gave a bark of derisive laughter.

'What planet are you living on, Sarah? If…if I am indeed a father, then do you really think I'm going to walk out on my responsibility? I will support you in every way that I can. What possible choice would I have?'

Tacked on at the end, that flat assertion said it all. He would rise to the occasion and do his duty. Having wanted nothing in life but to be free, he would now find himself chained to a situation from which he would never allow himself to retreat. She wondered if he had any idea how that made her feel, and felt painful tears push their way up her throat.

She found a clean white handkerchief pressed into her hand, and she stared down at the floor, blinking rapidly in an attempt to control her emotions. 'You never owned a hankie when I knew you,' she said in a wobbly voice, reaching for anything that might be a distraction from what she was feeling.

Raoul gave her a reluctant smile. 'I have no idea why I own one now. I never use it.'

'What about when you have a cold and need to blow your nose?'

'I don't get colds. I'm as healthy as a horse.'

It was only a few meaningless exchanged words, but Sarah felt a lot better as she stuck the handkerchief in the pocket of her overall, promising to return it when it had been washed.

'I'll need to be able to contact you,' he told her. 'What's your mobile number? I'll write mine down for you, and you can contact me at any time.'

As they exchanged numbers, she couldn't help but think back to when he had walked out on her with no forwarding address and no number at which he could be contacted. He had wanted to be rid of her completely—a clean cut, with no loose threads that could cause him any headaches later down the road.

'I'll be in touch within the week,' he told her, pocketing his mobile, and then he watched as she nodded silently and walked out of the room. He saw her yank off the overall and dump it in the trolley, along with the headscarf. She left it all just where it was in a small act of rebellion that brought a smile to his lips.

Alone in the office, and alone with his thoughts, Raoul contemplated the bomb that had detonated in his life.

He had a son.

Despite what he had said about wanting evidence, he knew in his gut that the child was his. Sarah had never cared about money, and she had always been the least manipulative woman he had ever known. He believed her when she said that she had tried to contact him, and he was shaken by the thought of her doing her utmost to bring up a child on her own when she had been just a child herself.

The fact was that he had messed up and he would have to pay the price. And it was going to be a very steep price.

CHAPTER TWO

SARAH was at the kitchen sink, finishing the last of the washing up, when the doorbell went.

The house she rented was not in a particularly terrific part of East London, but it was affordable, public transport was reasonably convenient, and the neighbours were nice. You couldn't have everything.

Before the doorbell could buzz again and risk waking Oliver, who had only just been settled after a marathon run of demands for more and more books to be read to him until finally he drifted off to sleep, Sarah wiped her hands on a dishcloth and half ran to the front door.

At not yet seven-thirty she was in some faded tracksuit bottoms and a baggy tee shirt. It was her usual garb on a weekend because she couldn't afford to go out. Twice a month she would try and have some friends over, cook them something, but continually counting pennies took a lot of the fun out of entertaining.

She had spent the past two days caught up in trying to find herself some replacement shift work. The cleaning company that had hired her had been appalled to find that she had walked out on a job without a backward glance, and she had been sacked on the spot.

Her heart hadn't been in the search, however. She'd been too busy thinking about Raoul and tirelessly replaying their unexpected encounter in her head. She'd spent hours trying to analyse what he had said and telling herself that it had all happened for the best. She'd looked at Oliver and all she'd seen was Raoul's dark hair and bitter chocolate eyes, and the smooth, healthy olive skin that would go a shade darker as he got older. He was a clone of his father.

If Raoul saw him there would be no doubt, but she still hadn't heard from him, and her disappointment had deepened with every passing hour.

On top of that, she couldn't make her mind up what she should tell her parents. Should they know that Raoul was Oliver's father and was back on the scene? Or would they worry? She had confessed that she had had her heart broken, and she wasn't convinced that they had ever really believed it to have been fully pieced together again. How would they react if they knew that the guy who'd broken her heart was back in her life? She was an only child, and they were super-protective. She imagined them racing up to London wielding rolling pins and threatening retribution.

She pulled open the door, her mind wandering feverishly over old ground, and stepped back in confusion at the sight of Raoul standing in front of her.

'May I come in, Sarah?'

'I...I wasn't expecting you. I thought you said that you were going to phone...'

She was without make-up, and no longer in a uniform designed to keep all hint of femininity at bay, and Raoul's dark eyes narrowed as he took in the creamy satin smoothness of her skin, the brightness of her green eyes in her heart-shaped face and the curves of her familiar body underneath her tee shirt and track pants.

He recognised the tee shirt, although it was heavily

faded now, its rock group logo almost obliterated. Just looking at it took him back in time to lying on the bed in the small room in Africa, with the mosquito net tethered as best they could manage under the mattress, watching and burning for her as she slowly stripped the tee shirt over her head to reveal her full, round breasts.

Raoul had planned on phoning. He had spent the past two days thinking, and had realised that the best way forward would be to view the situation in the same way he would view any problem that needed a solution—with a clear head. First establish firm proof that the child was his, because his gut instinct might well be wrong, and then have an adult conversation with her regarding the way forward.

Unfortunately he hadn't been able to play the waiting game. He hadn't been able to concentrate at work. He had tried to vent his frustration at the gym, but even two hours of gruelling exercise had done nothing to diminish his urgent need to *do something*.

Sarah read everything into his silence and ushered him into the house.

'I didn't know if I should be expecting a call from… somebody…about those tests you wanted…'

'On hold for the moment.'

'Really?' Her eyes shone and she smiled. 'So you *do* believe me.'

'For the moment I'm prepared to give you the benefit of the doubt.'

'You won't regret it, Raoul. Oliver's the image of you. I'm sorry he's asleep. I *would* wake him…'

Raoul had no experience of children. They weren't part of his everyday existence, and in the absence of any family he had never been obliged to cut his teeth on nephews or nieces. He was utterly bewildered at the notion of being in the presence of a son he had never laid eyes on. What did a four-year-old boy *do*, exactly? Were they capable of making conversation at that age?

Suddenly nervous as hell, he cleared his throat and waved aside her offer. 'Maybe it's best if we talk about this first...'

'Then would you like something to drink? Tea? Coffee? I think I might have some wine in the fridge. I don't keep a great deal of alcohol in the house. I can't afford it, anyway.'

Raoul was looking around him, taking in the surroundings which were a stark reminder of how far he had travelled. Now he lived in a massive two-storeyed penthouse apartment in the best postcode in London, furnished to the very highest standard. Frankly, it was the best that money could buy—although he barely glanced at his surroundings and was seldom in to take advantage of the top-of-the-range designer kitchen and all the other jaw dropping features the high-tech apartment sported.

This tiny terraced house couldn't have been more different. The carpet, the indeterminate colour of sludge, had obviously never been replaced, and the walls, although painted in a cheerful green colour, showed signs of cracks. Standing in the hall with her, he was aware there was practically no room to move, and as he followed her into the kitchen there was no change. A pine table was shoved against the wall to accommodate random pieces of free-standing furniture—a half-sized dresser, a chest of drawers, some shelves on which bottles with various cooking ingredients stood.

He had managed to climb up and away from these sorts of surroundings, but it still sent a chill through his body that but for a combination of brains, luck and sheer hard work beyond the call of duty he might very well have still been living in a place very much like this.

This was precisely why, he told himself, he had refused to be tied down. Only by being one hundred percent free to focus on his career had he been able to fulfil his ambitions. Women were certainly an enjoyable distraction, but he had never been tempted to jettison any of his plans for one of them.

The more wealth he accumulated, the more jaded he became. He could have the most beautiful women in the world, and in fact he had had a number of head-turning girlfriends on his arm over the years, but they had always been secondary to his career.

Dim memories of living in a dingy room with his mother while she drank herself into a stupor had been his driving force. This house was only a few steps up from dingy. He imagined the landlord to be someone of dubious integrity, happy to take money from desperate tenants, but less happy to make any improvements to the property.

The notion of *his son* had somehow managed to take root in his head, and Raoul was incensed at the deplorable living conditions.

'I know,' Sarah apologised, following the critical path of his eyes. 'It's not fantastic, but everything works. And it's so much better than some of the other places I looked at. I don't even know where *you* live...'

Raoul, who had been staring at a dramatic rip in the wallpaper above the dresser, met her eyes and held them.

He couldn't understand whether it was her familiarity that was making him feel so *aware of her*—inconveniently, frustratingly, *sexually* aware of her—or whether he had just managed to make himself forget the attraction she had always had for him.

'Chelsea,' he said grimly, sitting on one of the chairs

at the table, which felt fragile enough to break under his weight.

'And…and what's it like?' She could feel hot colour in her cheeks, because he just dominated the small space of the kitchen. His presence seemed to wrap itself around her, making her pulses race and her skin feel tight and uncomfortable.

Coffee made, she handed him a mug and sat on the other chair.

'It's an apartment.' He shrugged. 'I don't spend a great deal of time in it. It works for me. It's low maintenance.'

'What does that mean? Low maintenance?'

'Nothing surplus to requirements. I don't like clutter.'

'And…and is there a woman in that apartment?' She went bright red as she asked the question, but it was one that had only occurred to her after she had left him. Was there a woman in his life? He didn't give the impression of being a married man, but then would he ever?

'What's the relevance of that question?' He sipped some of the instant coffee and looked at her steadily over the rim of the mug.

'It's relevant to this situation,' she persisted stubbornly. 'Oliver's your son, and he's going to have to get used to the idea of having a father around. I'm the only parent figure he's ever known.'

'Which isn't exactly my fault.'

'I know it's not! I'm just making a point.' She glared at him. 'It's going to take time for him to get to know you, and I don't want him to have to deal with a woman on the scene as well. At least I'd rather not. I suppose if you're married…'

Having never had to answer to anyone but himself, Raoul refused to be railroaded into an explanation of his private life—although he could see the validity of her question.

'No. There's no little lady keeping the home fires burning. As for women... I'll naturally strive to ensure that a difficult situation isn't made even more difficult.'

'So there *is* someone.' She tried desperately to take it in her stride, because it really wasn't very surprising. He was sinfully gorgeous, and now wealthy beyond belief. He would be a magnet for any footloose and single woman— and probably for a good few who *weren't* footloose and single.

'I don't think we should get wrapped up in matters that don't really have much to do with this...situation. We just need to discuss what the next step should be.'

'Come upstairs and see him. I can't have this conversation with you when you don't even know the child you're talking about. This isn't a business deal that needs to be sorted out.' She stood up abruptly and Raoul, put on the spot, followed suit.

'He's sleeping. I wouldn't want you to wake him.' Raoul was more nervous than he could ever remember being— more nervous than when he had chased, and closed, his first major deal. More nervous than when he had been a kid and he had stared up at the forbidding grey walls of the foster home that would eventually become his residence.

'Okay. I won't. But you still have to see him, or else he's just going to be a *problem that needs solving* in your head.'

'Since when did you get so bossy?' Raoul muttered under his breath, and Sarah spun around to find him looming behind her.

Standing on the first stair, she could almost look him in the eye. 'Since I ended up being responsible for another human being,' she said. 'I know it's not your fault that you weren't aware of the situation…' *Although it was, because if he had only just given her a contact number she would have been able to get in touch with him.* 'But it was terrifying for me when I discovered that I was pregnant. I kept thinking how nice it would be if you had been around to support me, and then I remembered how you had dumped me because you had plans and they didn't include me, and that if you *had* been around my pregnancy would have been your worst nightmare.'

'My plans didn't include *anyone*, Sarah. I did you a favour.'

'Oh, don't be so arrogant! If you'd cared enough about me you would have kept in touch.' She was breathing heavily as all the remembered pain and bitterness and anger surged through her, but staring into the depths of his fabulous dark eyes was doing something else to her—making her whole body tingle as though someone had taken a powerful electrical charge to it.

Raoul clocked her reaction without even consciously registering it. He just knew that the atmosphere had become taut with an undercurrent that had nothing to do with what they had been talking about. It was a type of non-verbal communication that sent his body into crazy overdrive.

'I don't know why I'm bothering to tell you any of this.' She jerked her hand in clumsy dismissal, but he caught her wrist. The heat of physical contact made her draw in her breath sharply, although he wasn't hurting her—not at all. He was barely circling her wrist with his long fingers. Still…she was appalled to find that she wanted to sink against him.

That acknowledgment of weakness galvanised her into struggling to free herself and he released her abruptly, although when she could have turned around and stalked up the stairs she continued to stare at him wordlessly.

'I know it must have been a bad time for you...'

'Well, that's the understatement of the decade if ever there was one! I felt completely lost and alone.'

'You had your parents to help you.'

'That's not the same! Plus I'd left for my gap year thinking that I was at the start of living my own life. Do you know what it felt like to go back home? Yes, they helped me, and I couldn't have managed at all without them, but it still felt like a retrograde step. I never, ever considered having an abortion, and I was thrilled to bits when Oliver was born, but I was having to cope with seeing all my dreams fly through the window. No university, no degree, no teaching qualification. You must have been laughing your head off when you saw me cleaning floors in that bank.'

'Don't be ridiculous.'

'No? Then what *was* going through your head when you looked down at me? With a damp cloth in one hand and a cleaning bottle in the other, dressed in my overalls?'

'Okay. I was stunned. But then I started remembering how damned sexy you were, and thinking how damned sexy you still were—never mind the headscarf and the overalls...'

His words hovered in the air between them, a spark of conflagration just waiting to find tinder. To her horror, Sarah realised that she wanted him to repeat what he had just said so she could savour his words and roll them round and round in her head.

How could she have forgotten the way he had treated her? He might justify walking out on her as *doing her a favour*, but that was just another way of saying that he hadn't cared for her the way she had cared for him, and he hadn't been about to let a meaningless holiday romance spoil his big plans.

'I've come to realise that sex is very overrated,' Sarah said scornfully, and then flushed as a slow smile curved his beautiful mouth.

'Really?'

'I don't want to talk about this.' But she heard the tell-tale tremor in her voice and wanted to scream in frustration. 'It certainly has nothing to do with what's…what's happening now. If you follow me, I'll show you to Oliver's room.'

Raoul let the conversation drop. He was as astounded as she had been by his own genuine admission to her, and he was busily trying to work out how a woman he hadn't seen in years—a woman who, in the great scheme of things, had not really been in his life for very long—could still exercise such a powerful physical hold over him. It was as though the years between them had collapsed and disappeared.

But of course they hadn't, he reminded himself forcefully. Proof of that was currently asleep in a bedroom, just metres away from where they had been standing.

Upstairs, if anything, seemed more cramped than downstairs, with two small bedrooms huddled around a tiny bathroom which he glimpsed on his way to the box room on the landing.

She pushed open the door to the only room he had seen so far that bore the hallmark of recent decoration. A night-light revealed wallpaper with some sort of kiddy theme and basic furniture. A small bed, thin patterned curtains, a circular rug tucked half under the bed, a white chest of drawers, snap-together furniture, cheap but functional.

Raoul unfroze himself from where he was standing

like a sentinel by the doorway and took a couple of steps towards the bed.

Oliver had kicked off the duvet and was curled around a stuffed toy.

Raoul could make out black curly hair, soft chubby arms. Even in the dim light he could see that his colouring was a shade darker than his mother's—a pale olive tone that was all *his*.

In the grip of a powerful curiosity, he took a step closer to the bed and peered at the small sleeping figure. When it shifted, Raoul instantly took a step back.

'We should go—just in case we wake him,' Sarah whispered, tiptoeing out of the bedroom.

Raoul followed her. The palms of his hands felt clammy.

She had been right. He had a son. There had been no mistaking those small, familiar signs of a likeness that was purely inherited. He wondered how he could ever have sat in his office and concluded that he would deal with the problem with the cold detachment of a mathematician completing a tricky equation. He had a child. A living, breathing son.

The cramped condition of the house in which he was living now seemed grossly offensive. He would have to do something about that. He would have to do something about pretty much everything. Life as he knew it was about to change. One minute he had been riding the crest of a wave, stupidly imagining that he had the world in the palm of his hand, and the next minute the wave had crashed and the world he had thought netted was spinning out of control.

It was a ground-breaking notion for someone whose only driving goal throughout his life had been to remedy the lack of control he had had as a child by conquering the world. A tiny human being, barely three feet tall, had put paid to that.

'You're very quiet,' Sarah said nervously, as soon as they were out of earshot.

'I need a drink—and something stronger than a cup of coffee.'

The remnants of a bottle of wine were produced and poured into a glass. Sarah looked at him, trying to gauge his mood and trying to forget that moment of mad longing that had torn through her only a short while before on the staircase.

'You were right,' he said heavily, having drunk most of the glass in one go. 'I see the resemblance.'

'I knew you would. It'll be even more noticeable when you see him in the light. He's got your dark eyes as well. In fact, there's not much of me at all in him! That was the first thing Mum said when he was born… Would you like to see some of the drawings he's made? He goes to a play-group two mornings a week…I get help with that…'

'Help? What kind of help?' Raoul dragged his attention away from the swirling wine in his glass and looked at her.

'From the government, of course,' Sarah said, surprised. How on earth could she afford childcare otherwise, when she worked as a cleaner? On the mornings when Oliver was at nursery, she helped out at the school at which she was due to start work, but that was unpaid.

Raoul controlled his temper with difficulty. 'From the government?' he repeated with deadly cool, and Sarah nodded uneasily. 'Do you know what my aim in life was? My *only* aim in life? To escape the clutches of government aid and own my future. Now you sit here and tell me that you're *reliant* on government aid to get you through life.'

'You make it sound like a crime, Raoul.'

'For *me*, it's obscene!'

The force of his personality hit her like a freight train travelling at full speed, but she squared her shoulders and glared at him defiantly. If she allowed him to take control just this once then she would be dancing to his tune as and when he wanted her to. Hadn't she done enough of that years ago? And look where it had got her!

'And I can understand that,' Sarah told him evenly. 'I really can. But your past has nothing to do with my present circumstances. I couldn't afford to put Oliver into a private nursery,' she informed him bluntly. 'You'd be shocked at how little I earn. Mum and Dad supplement me, but every day's a struggle. It's all very well for you to sit there and preach to me about pride and ambition, but pride and ambition aren't very high up in the pecking order when you barely have enough money to put food on the table. So if I can get help with the nursery, then I'll take it.' She wished that she had had some wine as well, because she was in dire need of fortification. 'You were never such a crashing snob before, Raoul,' she continued bitterly. 'I can see that you've changed in more ways than one.'

'Snob? I think you'll find that that's the last thing I am!' He was outraged that she could hurl that accusation at him in view of his past.

'You've moved away from your struggling days of when we first met! I'll bet you can't even remember what it was like, darning those shorts of yours when they got ripped because you couldn't afford to chuck them out!'

'*You* darned them.' He looked at her darkly. He could remember her doing it as if it had been yesterday, swatting mosquitoes and moths away while outside a dull rumble of thunder had heralded heavy rain. She had looked like a girl in a painting, with her hair tumbling around her face as she frowned in concentration.

Sarah bit back the temptation to tell him what an idiot she had been, doing stuff like that, worshipping the ground he walked on, eager to do whatever he wanted.

'And I *haven't* forgotten my past,' he said grimly. 'It's always there at the back of my mind, like a stuck record.'

Her heart softened, but she held her ground with grim determination.

'I may not have planned for this, but I want you to know that things are going to change now. This place is barely fit for habitation!' He caught the warning look in her eyes and offered her a crooked smile. 'Okay. Bit of an exaggeration. But you get where I'm going. Whether you think I've become a monstrous snob or not, I can afford to take you away from here—and that's got to be my number one priority.'

'Your number one priority is getting to know Oliver.'

'I would prefer to get to know him in surroundings that won't challenge me every time I walk through the front door.'

Sarah sighed. It would certainly make life easier not having to worry so much about money. 'Okay. I take back some of the things I said. You haven't completely changed. You still think that you can get your own way all the time.'

'I know. It more than compensates for *your* indecision. Now, you could put up a brief struggle to hold on to your independence, maybe give me a little lecture on things being just perfect here, with your quaint, outdated kitchen furniture and the walls in need of plasterwork, but we both know that you can see my point of view. I can afford to take you out of this, and I consider it my duty to do so.'

The word *duty* lodged in her head like a burr, and she looked down at her anxiously clasped fingers. There was nothing like honesty to really hurt.

'What do you suggest?' she asked. 'Do I have any input

here? Or are you going to just walk all over me because you have lots of money and I have none?'

'I'm going to walk all over you because I have lots of money and you have none.'

'Not funny,' Sarah muttered, remembering his talent for defusing a situation with his sense of humour. Given the conditions years ago, when they had been cooped up on the compound, tempers had occasionally run high and this talent of his had been invaluable. Was he using it now just to get his own way? And did that matter anyway? The prospect of no longer having a daily struggle on her hands was like being offered manna from heaven.

'I intend to take my responsibilities very seriously, Sarah. I think you should know that. It would be very time-consuming to travel out here every time I wanted to see Oliver. Somewhere closer to where I live would be a solution.'

Now that they were discussing things in a more businesslike manner Sarah could actually focus on what was being said—as opposed to fighting to maintain her equilibrium, which showed threatening signs of wanting to fall apart.

'I feel as though I'm suddenly on a rollercoaster ride,' she confessed.

'Spare a thought for me. Whatever rollercoaster ride you're on, mine is bigger, faster, and I'm a hell of a lot less prepared for it than you are.'

And yet he was rising to the occasion. It didn't matter that the only reason they were now even having this conversation was because she had become a responsibility he couldn't shirk. He had taken it all in his stride in his usual authoritative way. That there was no emotion involved was something she would have to deal with. It wasn't his problem, and she wasn't going to let that get in the way of the relationship he had to build with his son.

'So we move to another place… There are still all sorts of other things that need sorting out. I'll have to try and explain to Oliver that he has a…a father. He's only young, though. I should warn you that it might not be that easy.'

'He's four,' Raoul pointed out with impeccable logic. 'He hasn't had time to build up any kind of picture for or against me.'

'Yes, but—'

'Let's not anticipate problems, Sarah.'

Now that he had surmounted the sudden bout of intense nervousness that had gripped him in the bedroom, Raoul was confident he would be able to get Oliver onside. Having had a life of grinding poverty, replete with secondhand clothes and secondhand books and secondhand toys, and frankly secondhand affection, he was beginning to look forward to giving his son everything that he himself had lacked in his childhood.

'We take things one at a time. First the house. Secondly, I suggest you try and explain my role to Oliver. Has he… has he ever asked about his father?'

'In passing,' Sarah admitted. 'When he's been to a birthday party and seen the other kids with their dads. Once when I was reading him a story.'

Raoul's lips thinned but he didn't say anything. 'You will obviously have to tell your parents that you are moving, and why. Will you tell them I'm on the scene? What my position is?'

'Maybe we shouldn't go there just yet,' Sarah said vaguely.

'I won't hide in the shadows.'

'I'm not sure they're going to be overjoyed that you're on the scene, actually.' She flushed guiltily as she remembered their distress when she had told them how she had fallen hard for a guy who had then chucked her. The hormones rushing through her body had made her all the more vulnerable and emotional, and she had spared nothing in her mournful, self-pitying account.

Honestly, she didn't think that Raoul was going to be flavour of the month if she produced him out of nowhere. But she knew that she would have to sooner or later. Her mum always phoned at least three times a week, and always had a chat with Oliver. Sarah wouldn't want her to find out via her grandchild that the heartbreaker and callous reprobate was now around.

'I'm getting the picture,' Raoul said slowly.

Sarah thought it better to move on quickly from that topic of conversation. 'I'm sure they'll be very happy.' She crossed her fingers behind her back. 'They're very conventional. They'll be delighted that Oliver will now have a father figure in his life.'

He stood up. 'I'll be in touch tomorrow. No—scrap that. I'll come by tomorrow afternoon so that I can be introduced to my son.'

The formality of that statement brought a rush of colour to Sarah's face, because it underlined his lack of enthusiasm for the place in which he now found himself.

'Should I buy him something special to wear?' she said tartly. 'I wouldn't want his appearance to offend you.'

'That's not helpful.'

'Nor is your approach to Oliver!' Tears stung the back of her eyes. 'How can you be so...so...*unemotional*? This wasn't how I ever thought my life would turn out. I always thought that I would fall in love and get married, and when a baby came along it would be a cause for celebration and joy. I never imagined that I would have a child with a man who wasn't even pleased to be a father!'

Raoul flushed darkly. What did she expect of him? He was here, wasn't he? Prepared to take on a task which had been sprung on him. Not only that, but she would be the recipient of a new house to replace her dismal rented accommodation, and also in the enviable position of never having to worry about money in her life again. Were hysterical accusations in order? Absolutely not!

He was very tempted to give her a checklist of all the things she should be thankful for. He settled for saying, in a cool voice, 'I've found that life has a funny way of not playing fair in the great scheme of things.'

'Is that all you have to say?' Sarah cried in frustration. 'Honestly, Raoul, sometimes I could…*hit you*!'

Her eyes were blazing and her hair was a tumbling riot of gold—and he felt a charge race through his system like an uncontrolled dose of adrenaline.

'I'm flattered that I still get you so worked up,' he murmured with husky amusement.

He couldn't help himself as he reached out and tangled his fingers in that hair. The contact was electric. He felt her response slam into him like a physical force and he revelled in the dark sexual hunger snaking through his body. *That* was something no amount of hard-headed logic or cool, calm reason could control.

Her lips had parted and her eyes were unfocused and half closed. Kissing her would halt all those crazy accusations in mid-flow. And he was hungry for her—hungry to remind himself of what her lips felt like.

'Don't you dare, Raoul…'

He pulled her towards him and noted, with a blaze of satisfaction, the unspoken invitation in her darkened eyes.

That first heady taste of him was intoxicating. Sarah moaned and pressed her hands against his chest. He had always been able to make her forget everything with a single touch, and her mind duly went blank. She forgot everything as her body curved sensuously against his, every bit of her melting at the feel of his swollen masculinity pushing against her, straining against the zipper of his trousers. Her breasts ached and she moved them against him, almost fainting at the pleasurable sensation of the abrasive motion on her sensitised nipples.

Raoul was the first to pull away.

'I shouldn't have done that.'

It took a few seconds for the daze in Sarah's head to clear, and then she snapped back to the horrified realisation that after everything she had been through, and hot on the heels of her really, *really* wanting to hit him, she had just *caved in*—like an addict who couldn't control herself. He had kissed her and all the hurt, anger and disappointment had disappeared. She had become a mindless puppet and five years had vanished in the blink of an eye.

'Neither of us should have…'

'Maybe it was inevitable.'

'What do you mean? What are you talking about?'

'You know what I'm talking about. This *thing* between us…'

'There's nothing between us!' Sarah cried, stepping back and hugging herself in an automatic gesture of self-defence.

'Are you trying to convince me or yourself?'

'Okay, maybe we just…just gave in to something *for the sake of old times*.' She took a deep breath. 'And now we've got that out of the way we can move on and…and…'

'Pretend it never happened?'

'Exactly! Pretend it never happened!' She took a few more steps back, but she thought that even if she took a million steps back and fled the country the after-effects of that devastating kiss would still be with her. 'This isn't

about *us*. This is about Oliver and your part in his life, so…
so…'

Raoul looked at her with a brooding intensity that made
her tremble. She didn't have a clue what was going on in
his head. He had always been very good at shielding his
thoughts when it suited him. She worked herself up into
a self-righteous anger, remembering how terrific he had
been at keeping stuff from her—like their lack of future—
until she had fallen for him hook, line and sinker. Never
again would she let him have that level of control!

'So just come here tomorrow. You can meet Oliver, and
we can work out some kind of schedule, and…then we can
both just get on with our own lives…'

CHAPTER THREE

By THE time the doorbell went the following afternoon Sarah hoped that she had risen above her physical weakness of the day before and reached a more balanced place. In other words sorted her priorities. Priority number one was Oliver, and she bracingly repeated to herself how wonderful it was that his father would now be there for him, willing to take on a parental role, whatever that might be. A full and frank discussion of that was high on her agenda. Priority number two, on a more personal level, was to make sure that she kept a clear head and didn't get lost in old feelings and memories.

She opened the door to a casually dressed Raoul.

'Oliver's in the sitting room, watching cartoons,' she said, getting down to business straight away.

Raoul looked at her carefully, and noted the way her eyes skittered away from his, the way she kept one hand on the doorknob, as though leaving her options open just in case she decided to shut the door in his face. In fact she had only half opened the door, and he peered behind her pointedly.

'Are you actually going to let me in, or do you want me to forge a path past you?'

'I just want to say that we'll really need to discuss… um…the practicalities of this whole situation…'

'As opposed to what?'

'I've been thinking, Raoul…'

'Dangerous,' Raoul said softly. She was in a pair of jeans and a tight tee shirt that reminded him a little too forcibly of the mysterious physical hold she still seemed to have over him. He had spent the night vainly trying to clear his head of images of her.

'I've been thinking that we should have as little to do with one another as possible. I don't want anything to happen between us. Been there, done that and have the tee shirt. The important thing is that you get to know Oliver, and that should be the extent of our relationship with one another.'

'And have you told him who I am?'

Sarah was startled and a little taken aback at the speed with which he had concluded a conversation she had spent hours rehearsing in her head. Had she hoped that he would at least try and knock down some of her defences? Had she erected her *Keep Off* sign in the expectation that he might just try and steamroller through it? Had she secretly *wanted* him to steamroller through it?

'Not yet,' she said crisply. 'I thought it best that you two get to know one another first.'

'Okay. Well, there's some stuff I'd like to bring in.'

'Stuff? What kind of stuff?'

He nodded to his car, which was parked a few spaces along. 'Why don't you go inside? I'll be a few minutes.'

'You haven't bought him presents, have you?' she asked suspiciously, but when she tried to step outside to get a closer look, he gently but firmly prevented her.

'Now, how did I know that you would disapprove?'

'It's not appropriate to show up with an armful of gifts the very first time you meet him!'

'I'm making up for lost time.'

Sarah gave up. You couldn't buy affection, she conceded, but perhaps a small token might help break the ice. Oliver had had no male input in his short life so far aside from her own father, whom he adored. She had been too busy just trying to make ends meet to dip her toes in the dating pool, and anyway she had not been interested in trying to replace Raoul. To her way of thinking she had developed a very healthy cynicism of the opposite sex. So Oliver's sole experience of the adult world, to a large extent, had been *her*.

He was in the process of trying to construct a tower of bricks, with one eye on the manic adventures of his favourite cartoon character, when Raoul appeared in the doorway. In one arm there was a huge box, and in the other an enormous sack.

There was more in the boot of the car, but Raoul just hadn't had the arms to bring it all in. Now he was glad that he hadn't. Oliver appeared to be utterly bewildered, and Sarah… Her mouth had fallen open in what could only be described as an expression of horror. Couldn't she say something?

Feeling like a complete fool for the first time in as long as he could recall, Raoul remained standing in the doorway with what he hoped was a warm smile pasted to his face.

'Oliver! This is…this is my friend, Raoul! Why don't you say hi to him?'

Oliver scuttled over to Sarah and clambered onto her lap, leaving Raoul trying to forge a connection by introducing a series of massively expensive presents to his son.

An oversized remote controlled car was removed from the box. The sack was opened to reveal a collection of games, books and stuffed toys which, Raoul assured a progressively more alarmed Sarah, had come highly recommended by the salesperson at the toy shop. He stooped to Oliver's level and asked him if he would care to try out the car. Oliver, by way of response, shook his head vigorously, to indicate very firmly that the last thing he wanted was to go anywhere near the aggressive silver machine that took up a fair amount of their sitting room space.

The games, books and stuffed toys garnered the same negative response, and silence greeted Raoul's polite but increasingly frustrated questions about playschool, sport and favourite television programmes.

At the end of an agonising forty-minute question and no answer session, Oliver finally asked Sarah if he could carry on with his blocks. In various piles lay the items that Raoul had bought, untouched.

'Well, *that* was a roaring success,' was the first thing Raoul muttered venomously under his breath, once he and Sarah were in the kitchen, leaving Oliver in the sitting room.

'It's going to take time.'

Raoul glared at her. 'What have you told him about me?'

'Nothing. Just that you were an old friend.'

'Hence the friendly way with in I was greeted?'

His own son had rejected him. Over the years, in his inexorable upward march, Raoul had trained himself to overcome every single setback, because every setback could be seen as a learning curve. He needed to speak French to close a deal? He learnt it. He needed intimate knowledge of the gaming market to take over a failing computer company? He acquired sufficient knowledge to get him by, and employed two formidable gaming geeks to do the rest. He had built an empire on the firm belief that he was capable of doing anything. There were no obstacles he was incapable of surmounting.

Yet half an hour in the company of a four-year-old had

rendered him impotent. Oliver had been uninterested in every toy pulled out of the bag and indifferent to *him*. There was no past experience upon which Raoul could call to get him through his son's lack of enthusiasm.

'Most kids would have gone crazy over that toy car,' he imparted in an accusatory tone. 'At least that's what the salesperson told me. It's been their biggest seller for the past four years. That damned car can do anything except carry passengers on the M25. So tell me what the problem was?' He glared at her as she serenely fetched two glasses from the cupboard and poured them some wine. 'The boy barely glanced in my direction.'

'I don't think it was such a good idea to bring so many toys for him.'

'And how do you work that one out? I would have been over the moon if I had ever, as a kid, been given *one* new toy! So how could several new, expensive, top of the range toys fail to do the trick?'

With a jolt of sympathy that ran contrary to every defence mechanism she had in place, Sarah realised that he really didn't have a clue. He had drawn from his own childhood experiences and arrived at a solution for winning his son's affections—except he hadn't realised that there was more to gaining love and trust than an armful of gifts.

'Do you know,' Raoul continued, swallowing the contents of his glass in one gulp, 'that every toy I ever played with as a child had come from someone else and had to be shared? A remote controlled car like the one languishing in your sitting room would have caused a full-scale riot.'

'That's just awful,' Sarah murmured.

'Now you're about to practise some amateur psychology on me. Don't. You should have told me that he liked building things. I would have come armed with blocks.'

'You're missing the point. You need to engage him. Like I said, he's used to only having me around. He's going to view any other adult on the scene with suspicion. What happened on birthdays? Christmas?'

'What are you talking about?'

'With you? Didn't you get birthday presents? What about Father Christmas?'

Raoul looked at her with a crooked smile that went past every barrier and settled somewhere in the depths of her heart.

'I don't see what this has to do with anything, but if you really want to know Father Christmas was tricky. Frankly, I don't think I ever believed in the fat guy with the beard. My earliest memory is of my mother telling me when I was three years old that there was no such person. Thinking about it now, I suspect she didn't want to waste valuable money on feeding that particular myth when the money could have been so much better spent on a bottle of gin. Anyway, even at the foster home there wasn't much room to hold on to stories like that. Father Christmas barely rated a mention.' He laughed without rancour. 'So—you're going to give me a lesson on engagement. If Oliver has no time for anything I bought for him, then how do we proceed?'

'Are you asking for my help?'

'I'm asking for your opinion. If I remember correctly, you have never been short of those...'

'Why don't you go out there and build something with him?' she suggested. 'No. I'll get him to bring his bricks in here, and the two of you can build something on the kitchen table while I prepare supper.'

'Forget about cooking. I'll take you both out. Name the restaurant and I'll ensure the chef is only too happy to whip up something for Oliver.'

'No,' Sarah said firmly. 'This is what normal life is all

about with a child, Raoul. Spaghetti Bolognese, familiar old toys, cartoons on television, reading books at night before sleep…' Except, she thought, suddenly flustered by the picture she had been busy painting, that was the *ideal* domestic situation—one in which two people were happily married and in love. It certainly wasn't *their* situation. As she had told him—*and she had meant every word of it*—they had no relationship outside the artificial one imposed by circumstance.

'Okay. I'll bring Oliver in and you can start chopping some onions. They're in the salad drawer in the fridge. Chop them really small.'

'You want me to *cook*?'

'Well, to help at any rate. And don't tell me that you've forgotten how to cook. You used to cook on the compound.'

'Different place, different country.'

'So…you just eat out all the time?' Sarah asked, distracted.

'It's more time-efficient.'

'And what about with your girlfriends? Don't you want to stay in sometimes? Do normal stuff?'

The questions were out before she had the wit to keep her curiosity to herself, and now that she had voiced them, she realised that it had been on her mind, poised just beneath the surface, ever since she had laid eyes on him again. In fact, thinking about it, it was something she had asked herself over and over again through the years. Had he found someone else? Had another woman been able to capture his interest sufficiently for him to make the commitment that he had denied her? He hadn't loved *her*, but had he fallen in love with someone else? Someone prettier or cleverer or more accomplished?

'Not that it's any of my business,' she added, and laughed airily.

'It is now. Haven't you said that yourself? No women in Oliver's presence… Rest assured that the only woman in my life at the moment is *you*…'

'That's not what I was asking and you know it, Raoul!'

'No. You're just curious to know what I've been getting up to these past few years. There's nothing wrong with curiosity. Curiosity's healthy.'

'I don't *care* what you've been getting up to!' It was a lie. She cared. Who were these women he had dated? What had he felt for them? Anything? Had he preferred them to *her*? She was mortified just thinking about that particular question.

'I haven't been getting up to anything of interest,' Raoul replied drily. 'Yes, there have been women. But I've deterred them from doing anything that involved pots, pans, an apron, candlelight and home-cooked food.'

'Oh, Raoul, you're such a charmer.' But a tendril of relief curled inside her. She squashed it. 'Now, I'm going to fetch Oliver.'

'Hey, what about you? Don't I get the low-down on *your* life? No man at the moment, but any temptations? Do you cook your spaghetti Bolognese for anyone else aside from Oliver?'

His voice was light and mildly amused, and he wondered why he felt so tense when it came to thinking of her with another man. He, after all, had never been and would never be a candidate when it came to marriage and rings on fingers. He was now a father, and that was shocking enough, but that was the only derailment to his carefully constructed life on the cards as far as he was concerned.

'Maybe…'

'Maybe? What does *that* mean?' The amusement sounded forced. 'Am I in competition with someone you've got hidden in a cupboard somewhere?'

'No,' Sarah admitted grudgingly. 'I've been too busy being a single mum to think of complicating my life with a guy.' She sensed rather than saw the shadow of satisfaction cross his face, and continued tartly, 'But, as you've pointed out, life is going to get much easier for me now. It's going to make a huge difference with you around, playing a role in Oliver's life. I won't be doing it on my own. Also, it'll be nice not having to think about money, or rather the lack of it, all the time—and it'll be fantastic having a bit of time to myself…time to do what I want to do.'

'Which *doesn't* mean that you've now got carte blanche to do whatever you like.' Raoul didn't care for the direction in which this conversation was now travelling.

'You make me sound like the sort of girl who can't wait to pick someone up!'

She was wondering what right he had to lay down any kind of laws when it came to her private life. Raoul Sinclair didn't want his life encumbered with attachments. True, he had discovered that some encumbrances were beyond his control, but just as he had never contemplated committing to her, so he had never contemplated committing to anyone. It was small comfort. *He* might think that it was perfectly acceptable to lead a life in which he and his son were the only considerations, but it was totally unfair to assume that *she* felt the same way. *He* might want to pick up women and discard them when they were no longer of any use, but *she* needed more than that. For Raoul, a single life was freedom. For her, a single life would be a prison cell.

'I'm not going to suddenly start scouring the nightclubs for eligible men,' she expanded, with a bright, nervous laugh, 'but I *will* be able to get out a bit more—which will be nice.'

'Get out a bit more?'

'Yes—when you have Oliver.'

'I don't think we should start projecting at this point,' Raoul said deflatingly. 'Oliver hasn't even spoken to me as yet. It's a bit premature to start planning a hectic social life in anticipation of us becoming best friends. Let's just take one day at a time, shall we?'

'Of course. I wasn't planning on going clubbing next week!'

Clubbing? What did she mean by that? Other men? Sleeping around? While he kept Oliver every other weekend?

He pictured her dressed in next to nothing, flaunting herself on a dance floor somewhere. Granted, the women he went out with often dressed in next to nothing, but for some reason the thought of *Sarah* in a mini-skirt, high heels and a halterneck top set his teeth on edge.

'Good. Because it won't be happening.'

'Excuse me?'

'Think about it, Sarah. Oliver doesn't even know that I'm his father. Don't you think that he'll be just a little bit confused if *your friend*, who has mysteriously and suddenly appeared on the scene from nowhere, starts engineering outings without you? You're the constant in his life. As you keep telling me. For me to have any chance of being accepted we have to provide a united front. We have to get to a point where he trusts me enough to leave you behind now and again.'

'Exactly what are you trying to say, Raoul?'

'That you have to scrap any crazy notions of us having nothing to do with one another. You're living in cloud cuckoo land if you think that's going to work. The whole bedtime story, spaghetti Bolognese thing is going to have to involve both of us. Of course it'll be a damn sight easier when you get out of this place and move somewhere more

convenient. And less cramped. On the subject of which—
I have my people working on that.'

There were so many contentious things packed into that
single cool statement that Sarah looked at him, staggered.

'When you say *involve both of us*...'

Raoul flushed darkly and dealt her a fulminating look
from under his lashes.

'I don't know the first thing about being a parent,' he
told her roughly. 'You've witnessed my sterling performance out there.'

'I didn't know the first thing about being a parent either,' Sarah pointed out with irrefutable logic. 'It's just a
case of doing your best.'

The thought of doing things with Raoul and Oliver, a
cosy threesome, was enough to bring on the beginnings
of a panic attack in her. Already she was finding it difficult to separate the past from the present. She looked at
him, and who was she kidding when she told herself that
she was no longer attracted to him? Raoul was in a different place, and would be able to take her on board as just a
temporary necessity in his life, easily set aside once he had
what he wanted: some sort of ongoing relationship with
his son. But she was aghast at the prospect of having him
there in *her* life. How on earth was she ever going to get
to that controlled, composed place of detachment if she
was continually tripping over him in the kitchen as he attempted to bond with his son over fish fingers?

Perhaps he had exaggerated, she thought, soothing her
own restless, panicked mind. He was still smarting from
Oliver's less than exuberant reception of him. Right at this
very moment this was the only plan he could see ahead of
him, and Raoul was big on plans. He would not be taking
into account the simple fact that when children were involved plans could never really be made. In a day or two

he would probably revise his ideas, because she very much doubted that he wanted to spend quality time with *her* in the picture.

'And the whole house issue...' she continued faintly. 'You have your *people* working on it?'

'Here's one of the things I've discovered about having money: throw enough of it at a problem and the problem goes away. Right now they're in the process of drawing up lists of suitable properties. I will be giving them until the end of next week. So,' he drawled when she failed to respond, 'are we on the same wavelength here, Sarah?'

'I can't just move into a house *you* happen to choose. I know you probably don't care about your surroundings, but *I* care about mine...'

'Don't you trust me to find somewhere you'd like?'

He'd used to be amused at her dreamy, whimsical ideas. From where he had stood there had been little use for dreams unless you had the wherewithal to turn them into reality, and even then he had never made the mistake of confusing dreams with the attainment of real, concrete goals. What was the point in wishing you could own a small island in the middle of the Pacific if the chances of ever having one were zero? But her dreams of cottages and clambering roses and open fires had made him smile.

'True, the thatched cottage with the roses and the apple trees might be a little troublesome to find in London...'

Sarah blushed, unsettled by the fact that he had remembered her corny youthful notion of the perfect house. Which she recalled describing in tedious detail.

'But I've got them working on the Aga in the kitchen, the garden overlooking water, and the fireplaces...'

'I can't believe you remember that conversation!'

She gave a brittle laugh, and went an even brighter

shade of red when he replied softly, 'Oh, there's a lot I remember, Sarah. You'd be surprised.'

He didn't miss the flare of curiosity in her eyes. She might have made bold statements about not wanting anything to do with him, about shoving that kiss they had shared into a box at the back of a cupboard in her head, where she wouldn't have to confront it, but every time they were in each other's company he could feel that undercurrent of electricity—a low, sizzling hum that vibrated just below the radar.

'Well, I don't actually remember all that much,' Sarah responded carelessly.

'Now, I wonder why I'm not believing you…'

'I have no idea, and I don't care. Now, if you wouldn't mind getting to work on those onions, I'll go and fetch Oliver.'

She disappeared before he could continue the conversation. When he looked at her like that she would swear that he could see right down into the very depths of her. It was an uncomfortable, frightening sensation that left her feeling vulnerable and exposed. Once she had gladly opened up to him—had told him everything there was to know about herself. She had taken him at face value and turned a blind eye to the fact that while she had been falling deeper and deeper in love with him, he had pointedly refused to discuss anything that involved a future between them. He had taken everything she had so generously given and then politely jettisoned her when his time on the compound was up.

Raoul was a taker, with little interest in giving back. When he looked at her with those lazy, brooding eyes she could sense his interest. Some of his remarks carried just that little hint of flirtation, of deliberately treading very close to the edge. He had possessed her once, much to her shame. Did he think that he could possess her again?

She returned with Oliver to find him at the kitchen counter, dutifully chopping the onions as instructed.

Oliver had brought in a handful of his blocks, and Sarah sat him on a chair and then called Raoul over. She made sure to keep her voice light and friendly, even though every nerve in her body tingled as he strolled towards them, a teatowel draped over one shoulder.

'Blocks…my favourite.'

She had sat at the table, next to Oliver, and now Raoul leaned over her, his strong arms trapping her as he rested his hands on the table on either side of her. Sarah could feel his breath whisper against her neck when he spoke.

'Did you hear that, Oliver? Raoul loves building things! Wouldn't it be fun for you two to build something for me? What about a tower? You love building towers! Do you remember how high your last tower was? Before it fell?'

'Twelve blocks,' Oliver said seriously, not looking at Raoul. 'I can count to fifty.'

'That's quite an achievement!' Raoul leaned a little closer to Sarah, so that the clean, minty smell of her shampoo filled his nostrils.

She shifted, but had almost no room for manoeuvre. Her eyes drifted compulsively to his forearm, to the fine sprinkling of dark hairs that curled around the dull matt silver of his mega-expensive watch.

'Why don't you sit down, Raoul?' she suggested stiltedly. 'You can help Oliver with his tower.'

'I don't need any help, Mum.'

'No, he really doesn't. I sense that he's more than capable of building the Empire State Building all on his own.'

Oliver glanced very quickly at Raoul, and then returned to the task in hand.

Sarah heard Raoul's almost imperceptible indrawn breath as he abruptly stood back, and when she turned to look at him he had removed himself to the kitchen sink, his expression one of frustrated defeat.

'Give it time,' she said in a low voice, moving to stand in front of him.

'How much time? I'm not a patient man.'

'Well, I guess you'll have to learn how to be. Good job with the onions, by the way.'

But she could feel his simmering impatience with the situation for the rest of the evening. Oliver was not so much hostile as wary. He answered Raoul's questions without meeting his eye and, dinner over, finally agreed to go outside with him to test drive the car which had been abandoned in the sitting room.

Through the kitchen window, Sarah watched their awkward interaction with a sinking heart.

She had planned on sitting Oliver down and explaining that Raoul was his father once a bond of trust between them had been accepted. To overload him with too much information would be bewildering for him. But how long was that going to take? she wondered. Raoul was obviously trying very hard.

She watched as Oliver sent the oversized car bouncing crazily into the unkempt bushes at the back of the tiny garden, losing interest fast and walking away as Raoul stooped down to deliver a mini-lecture on mechanics.

The consequences of him missing out, through no fault of his own, on those precious first four years hit her forcibly. Another man, with experience of growing up in a real family, might have had something to fall back on in a situation like this. Raoul had no such experience, and was struggling to find a way through his own shortcomings.

She abandoned her plans to have him read something to

Oliver before bed, which was their usual routine. Instead, she told him to wait for her in the kitchen while she settled Oliver.

'You can help yourself to…um…whatever you can find in the fridge. I know dinner was probably not what you're used to…'

'Because I'm such a snob?'

Sarah sighed heavily, 'I'm just conscious that we're… we're miles apart. When we were working out in Africa there wasn't this great big chasm separating us…'

'You need to move on from the past.'

'*You* haven't moved on from yours!'

'I'm not following you?'

'You thought you could buy Oliver with lots of presents because that's what your past has conditioned you to think! And then you got impatient when you discovered that it doesn't work that way.'

'And *you* can't move on from the fact that—okay… yes—I dumped you!' Raoul thundered. 'You want to find something to argue about—*anything at all*—because you've wrapped yourself up in a little world comprised of just you and Oliver and you can't deal with the fact that I'm around now! Dinner was disappointing because it was stressful! I didn't know how to deal with him.'

Hell, Oliver had played with his food, spread most of it on the table, and had received only the most indulgent scolding from Sarah! His childhood memories of mealtimes were of largely silent affairs, with rowdy behaviour at the table meriting instant punishment.

'I *don't* know how to deal with him.'

Dumbfounded by that raw admission, Sarah was overcome with regret for her outburst. He was so clever, so *all-knowing*, that she hadn't really stopped to consider that now he really was at a loss.

'I'm…I'm sorry, Raoul. I shouldn't have said that stuff about your past…' she mumbled.

'Look, we've found ourselves in this situation, and constantly sniping isn't going to get either of us very far.'

Mind made up, Sarah nodded in agreement. 'I'll take him up for a bath… Yes, you're right…it's difficult for both of us…' She managed a smile. 'I guess we both need to do some adjusting…'

She returned forty-five minutes later and looked as fresh as a daisy. He felt as though he had done ten rounds in a boxing ring.

'I think he's really beginning to warm to you!' she said cheerfully.

Raoul raised his eyebrows in an expression of rampant scepticism. 'Explain how you've managed to arrive at that conclusion?' He raked his fingers through his hair and shook his head with a short, dry laugh. 'There's no need to put on the Little Miss Sunshine act for me, Sarah. I may not know much when it comes to kids, but I'd have to have the IQ of a goldfish not to see that my own son has no time for me. You were right. All those toys were a complete waste of time and money.'

'You're just not accustomed to children. You don't know how they think. Sometimes it's hard to imagine you being a kid at all! Oliver enjoys pushing the boundaries. Most children do, Raoul. He'll fiddle with his food until I have to be firm, and he'll always go for *just another five minutes* or *one more story* or *two scoops of ice cream, please*.'

'Whatever happened to discipline?' Raoul scowled at her laid-back attitude.

'Oh, there's a lot of that. It's just knowing when to decide that it's really needed.'

She looked at Raoul thoughtfully. The man who could move mountains had discovered his Achilles' heel, and she was sure that he would never ask for her help. He was stubbornly, maddeningly proud. To ask for help would be to admit a weakness, and she knew that was something he would find it very hard to do.

But helping him was the only solution—and, more than that, helping him would give her a psychological boost, even out the playing field.

'Okay, well, he's now thrilled with the car. Tonight I'll pack away all the rest of the stuff you brought for him. I can bring bits out now and again as treats.' She folded her arms and braced herself to take control with a guy who was so used to having the reins that he probably had no idea relinquishing them was a possibility.

Raoul sat back and clasped his hands behind his head. He had thought for one crazy moment, when he had laid eyes on her again, that time hadn't changed her. He had been wrong. This was no longer the blindly adoring girl who had yielded to him with such abundant generosity. There was a steely glint in her eye now, and he realised that he had seen it before but maybe hadn't really recognised it for what it was. The molten charge between them was still there, whether she wanted to admit it or not, but along with that was something else...

Raoul felt a certain fascination, and a surge of raw, powerful curiosity.

'Am I about to get a ticking off?' he drawled, his eyes roving lazily over her from head to toe in a way that made it difficult for her not to feel frazzled.

'No,' she said sweetly. 'But I am going to tell you what you need to do, and you're going to listen to me.' She smiled a bit more when she saw his frown of incomprehension. 'You like to think you know everything, but you don't.'

'Oh? You're going to be my teacher, are you?'

'Whether you like it or not!'

Raoul shot her a slow, dazzling smile. 'Well, now,' he said softly, instantly turning the tables on her, 'it's been a while since anyone taught me anything. You might find that I like it a lot more than you expect…'

CHAPTER FOUR

SARAH looked at her reflection in the mirror and frowned. Her cheeks were flushed, and her eyes were glowing. She looked *excited*. Guilt shot through her, because this was just what she didn't want. She didn't *want* to find herself giddy with anticipation because Raoul was on his way over.

For the past four weeks she had kept her manner brisk and impersonal. She had pretended not to notice those occasional sidelong glances of his, when his fabulous dark eyes would rest speculatively on her face. She had taken extra care to downplay what she wore. Anyone would have been forgiven for thinking that the only components of her wardrobe were faded jeans, tee shirts, shapeless jumpers and trainers. Now that the weather was getting warmer, and spring was edging tentatively into summer, the jumpers had been set aside, but the jeans, the tee shirts and the trainers were still fully in evidence.

Sarah was determined to make sure that her relationship with Raoul remained detached and uninvolved. She knew that she couldn't afford to forget what had happened in the past.

She had thrown herself into the task of helping him get to know his son, and she had to admit that it was no longer the uphill struggle it had initially been. Oliver was gradually opening up and losing some of his restraint, and Raoul, in turn, was slowly learning how to relate to a child. Like a teacher struggling with troublesome pupils and finally seeing the light at the end of the tunnel, she could now cautiously tell herself that her role of mediator had been successful.

And *that* accounted for the glow in her eyes and her flushed cheeks.

Oliver was actually looking forward to seeing Raoul. In fact, he was dressed and ready to go.

She clattered down the stairs as the doorbell buzzed and smiled at the sight of Oliver in the sitting room, kneeling on the chair by the bay window, eyes peeled for Raoul's arrival. He had been treated to several rides in Raoul's sports car, and had gravely told her that he would buy *her* one just as soon as he had saved enough money. He had two pounds, and considered himself well on the way.

'Am I dressed correctly for a day out at a theme park, Miss?' Raoul laughed at her exasperated expression.

'You know I hate it when you call me that.'

'Of course you don't! It makes you feel special. And besides…I enjoy watching the way you blush when I say it.'

On cue, Sarah felt her cheeks pinken.

'You shouldn't say stuff like that.'

'Why not?'

'Because…because…it's not appropriate…'

And because it threatened her. She had been walking on thin ice for the past four weeks as he dug deeper and deeper under her defences with his easy charm, his wit, his willingness to tackle head-on a situation that must have rocked his world. She desperately wanted her one-dimensional memory of him back, because it was so much easier to deal with him as the man who had ruined her life.

'Now you really *are* beginning to sound like a school-teacher,' Raoul said softly. 'Should I expect to be punished any time soon?'

'Stop it!'

He held up his hands in a gesture of surrender and laughed, throwing his head back, keeping his velvety black eyes on her face.

Sarah glared at him. This couldn't continue. Raoul didn't know what he was doing to her, but she was mentally and emotionally exhausted. She would talk to Raoul today. Begin the process of sorting out visiting arrangements. She couldn't foresee any problem with Raoul now taking Oliver out for the day without her having to be there as chaperone.

In other words it was time to acknowledge that her brief stint at usefulness was over and Raoul had been right. It had been essential for them to present a united front to Oliver so that his confidence in Raoul could be built. Would it come as a shock for him to accept Raoul as his father? Certainly it would be a lot easier now than it would have been a month ago, when Raoul had been an intimidating stranger bearing expensive gifts who had landed in their midst from nowhere.

The gifts had all been stowed away and Raoul had not repeated his mistake—although he warned her he would definitely be christening the new house he had bought for them with something spectacular in the back garden.

When Sarah considered the speed with which her life had changed in a matter of a month, her head spun.

Raoul back on the scene. Oliver slowly beginning to bond with his father. A house which she and Oliver had seen only two weeks previously immediately purchased by Raoul on the spot, with enough money thrown at the deal to ensure that it closed with record speed.

'You like it. Why hang around?'

He had shrugged with such casual dismissal of the cost that Sarah had stared at him, open-mouthed. That had been the point when she had thought that the attainment of wealth was the most important thing to Raoul, and instinctively she had shied away from what that implied about his character. Very quickly, however, she had realised that the only thing wealth represented to him was freedom. Money gave him the ability to do as he liked without reference to anyone else. It was the opposite of the way he had grown up.

In fact, and only by accident, she had recently discovered that he gave large sums of his vast fortune to charity—including the very same charity which had originally brought them together all those years ago. She had been in his penthouse with Oliver, waiting for him while he finished a conference call in his office. Oliver had been wandering around, gaping at the high-tech television and then experimenting with the chrome and black leather stools at the granite-topped kitchen counter, swivelling round and round with childish enjoyment, and there on the table by the massive window that overlooked a private park had been a letter of gratitude, thanking Raoul for his contributions over the years.

Sarah had not mentioned a word of what she had inadvertently seen, but she had filed it away in her head, where it jostled for space with all the other bits and pieces she was unconsciously gathering about him. In every way he was the most complex man she would ever meet. He was driven, ambitious, and ferociously single-minded. But the way in which he had applied himself to the task of getting to know his son showed compassion, patience, and an ability to roll with the punches.

There was no question that he used women, and yet

there was nothing manipulative about him. He had big *Keep Out* signs all around him, and yet she couldn't help feeling that she had seen something of the boy who had become the man—even though when he talked about his past it was only through necessity, and in a voice that was utterly devoid of emotion.

Five years on and Raoul Sinclair still fascinated her. Although that was something that Sarah barely recognised. She just knew that she was becoming dangerously addicted to his visits, which were frequent, even though she kept telling him that she didn't want to disrupt his work schedule.

She felt as though she was seeing him through the eyes of an adult as opposed to the romantic young girl she had once been, and she wondered what life would be like when their relationship became normalised. When he popped over on a Wednesday evening and took Oliver out, leaving her behind, or when he had Oliver for a weekend and she had her much espoused free time to do as she liked.

She immediately told herself that it would be brilliant. She would be able to build some kind of life for herself! She no longer had the excuse of lack of money, lack of time and lack of opportunity.

Raoul had insisted on opening a bank account for her, and when she had tried to assert her independence he had turned her determination on its head by quietly telling her that it was the very least he could do, bearing in mind that she had been a single mother for all those years when he had been rapidly building his fortune. Had he been more aggressive she would have taken refuge in an argument. But, brilliant judge of character that he was, he had known the most efficient way to get exactly what he wanted.

Sarah sighed and tried not to think. Aside from the disturbing melee of her own feelings, there was the very simple reality that they would be moving soon, and Oliver would need to be told who Raoul really was.

Today they were going to a theme park. Oliver had never been to a theme park. Nor had Raoul. She had only learned this after a great deal of questioning, during which she had been determined to prise from him what he had longed for as a kid but never had. She had asked him in the crisp voice she made sure to use in order to reinforce that their relationship was entirely impersonal, and he had adopted the slightly sardonic, lazy drawl which he always used when referring to his past. But then he had said, in a voice that contained a certain amount of surprise—maybe because the memory had come from nowhere—that he had missed the big annual treat of the year when he had been nine years old and his age group were taken to a theme park. It had been a celebration of sorts, to mark the fiftieth anniversary of the place, but he had been laid up with flu and had spent the entire weekend cooped up in the sick quarters.

There and then Sarah had decided that a visit to the theme park was essential.

Lagging behind as Raoul and Oliver walked towards the car, Sarah mentally took in the picture they made. Raoul literally towered over his son, who had to walk at a smart pace to keep up with him. From behind, she noted the similarity of their hair colour and the trace of olive in Oliver's skin tone that would burnish and darken over time—just as Raoul's had. Oliver was proudly carrying his backpack, which was a new purchase, and wearing his jeans, also a new purchase.

Her eyes drifted across to Raoul and she felt suddenly dizzy, because he just continued to take her breath away. Without fear of being observed *watching him*, she feasted on the length of his muscular legs, the low-slung faded black jeans, the white shirt, sleeves slightly pushed up even though it was still quite cool. However good she was at being adult and detached when she was in his company, she still knew that her indifference was a long way from being secure.

Raoul popped the boot of his car and Sarah glanced in and said, surprised, 'What's all that?'

Raoul gazed down at her upturned face and shot her a crooked half-smile.

'What does it look like?'

'You've made a *picnic*?'

'*I* haven't made a picnic. My caterer has. I've been assured that there's an ample selection.'

The past few weeks had been a massive learning curve for Raoul. Having never seen himself in the role of father, he had found himself having to adapt in all sorts of ways that were alien to him. Defined through his staggering ability to work, he had had to sideline hours in front of his computer or at the office in favour of the soul-destroying task of trying to edge responses out of his son. Accustomed to having every word he spoke treated with respect, and every order he gave obeyed to the letter, he had had to dig deep and find levels of patience that were foreign to him—because small children frequently disobeyed orders and often lacked focus. Ferociously against ever asking anyone for help, he had found himself in the uncustomary position of having to take guidance from Sarah, so that his path to a relationship with Oliver was eased. He had had to learn how to jettison his very natural inclination to command. But it had all paid enormous dividends because Oliver was gradually warming to him.

And alongside that he'd been witness to a new side of Sarah, so wildly different from the impressionable young girl she had been years ago. There was a core of strength in her now that intrigued him.

'I'm impressed, Raoul,' Sarah murmured, staring down at the wicker basket and the requisite plaid rug, and the cooler which was full of ice-cold drinks.

She imagined that when he decided on a certain course of action he gave one hundred percent of his energy to it. His course of action, in this instance, was winning over the son he'd never known he had, and he had approached the task in hand with gusto. This elaborate picnic was evidence of that. All kids loved a picnic. *She* loved a picnic.

He slammed shut the boot on Sarah's dismayed realisation that in the process of charming Oliver Raoul had inadvertently been doing exactly the same with her.

'Of course I would have been more impressed if you'd prepared it all yourself…' Her voice sounded forced.

'Never satisfied…' But he was grinning in a way that made her skin warm. 'You're a tough taskmaster.'

'You don't need a caterer to prepare food for you. I know that you're perfectly capable of doing it yourself.'

'I'll bear that in mind for next time,' Raoul murmured.

'Next time? There won't be a next time,' she told him in a fast rush. 'Don't forget that all of this is…you know… part and parcel of your learning curve.'

'Theme park—tick. Picnic—tick. Homecooked food eaten at the kitchen table—tick. Fast food restaurant— tick. When did you get so regimented?'

'I'm not regimented. I'm practical. And isn't it time we left? Oliver's already in the car. Have I told you how excited he was about today? He could hardly get to sleep last night!'

'I found sleeping pretty difficult myself.'

Sarah's eyes widened, and she sucked in a shaky breath

as he braced himself against the car, circling her so that she had to half sit on the bonnet.

'What are you doing?' she squeaked.

'I'm tired of trying to kid myself that I don't want you, Sarah.'

'You *don't* want me. I don't want *you*. I know we've been getting along, but it's all because of Oliver—because… because… Don't look at me like that!' But her body was betraying her protest. 'This isn't part of the plan. You *like* plans. Have you forgotten?'

'Which just goes to show what a changed man I'm becoming.'

'You haven't changed, Raoul.' She flattened her hand against his chest to push him back, but just touching him weakened her defences. 'I told you—we've been there. We're not good for one another. We just need to be…to be friends…'

'Okay.' He straightened, and his voice was mild, but there was a glitter in his eyes that made her pulses race. 'If you're sure about that…'

He let his hand slide over her shoulder in a caressing, assured move that made her stomach flip and her breath catch in her throat. Then he backed off, and she was gulping in oxygen like a drowning person breaking the surface of the water.

Her heart was beating madly as she slipped into the passenger seat and turned to make sure that Oliver was strapped into his car seat. Over the years, her memories of Raoul had taken on a static form. Faced once again with the living, breathing, charismatic, dynamic and unbearably sexy Raoul, who could make her laugh and make her want to grind her teeth together in frustration in the next breath, had undermined all her defences.

Had he intuited this? Was that why he had made that

move? With the confidence of a predator knowing that it was just a matter of time?

The theme park was already packed by the time they got there. Oliver's excitement had been a slow burn, but his first sight of some of the rides, the chaos of the crowds, and the roar of the machines flying through the air with people dangling from them like rag dolls took his breath away.

'Does this live up to expectations?' Sarah asked Raoul halfway through, as he and Oliver descended from one of the child and parent rides. She was determined to keep her head and be as normal as possible. She *wouldn't* get in a flap.

It had warmed up, and his polo shirt exposed strong, muscled arms. She watched them flex and harden as he stooped to lift Oliver in one easy movement.

'Are you asking whether I've managed to discover my inner child yet? Nope,' he told her before she could say anything. 'I'm not one of those losers who gets wrapped up in that sort of thing.'

But, hell, he'd been doing quite a lot that was out of character for him. A picnic? Since when had he ever been the sort of guy who was interested in picnics? It was even more disquieting to realise that he had done it *for her*.

'Well, you should be.' Sarah saw a golden opportunity to strike out for independence and remind him that she had a life outside his many visits—that he couldn't just re-enter her life and take what he happened to want because it suited him.

Or maybe, she decided uneasily, it was to remind *herself* that she shouldn't be up for grabs, that she had a life outside his many visits. Although where exactly that life was she wasn't quite sure. The teaching assistant job which she had been due to start was now off the cards as they would be moving from the area, and she was caught in a limbo of not really knowing when she should start looking for something else. Should she wait until they had settled in their new house before she began registering with agencies?

With nothing on the agenda, it had been easy to slip into a comfortable pattern of just Oliver and Raoul. Really, it wasn't healthy.

'I mean,' she continued, as they began walking towards the next bank of rides. 'I don't think it's so much about getting in touch with your *inner child*. I think it's more about just being able to relax and have fun. I know you've been around us a lot, but that's not going to last for ever, and when you resume your hectic work schedule... Well, I can't imagine that you won't be stressed out. Having fun and taking time out can't be shoved into a few weeks before normal life resumes...'

'Why are you trying to engage me in an argument?'

'I'm just saying that there's nothing loser-like about someone who knows how to have a good time. In fact, I think it's a great quality in a guy. I'd go so far as to say that the kind of guy I would be interested in dating would be someone who really knew how to let his hair down and enjoy himself...'

When she tried to imagine this fictitious person, the image of Raoul annoyingly superimposed itself in her mind.

Raoul frowned and cast her a quelling look from under his lashes. He'd thought the subject of this so-called single life she envisaged leading had taken a back seat. He'd concluded that the matter had been shelved because she had seen the obvious—which was that there would be no single life for her while they were trying to sort out things with Oliver. It was disconcerting to think that she might have been biding her time, filling her head with thoughts of climbing back on the dating bandwagon when she was still attracted to *him*. He had *felt* it.

'Oliver's looking tired. I think we should have something to eat now,' he said coolly, turning abruptly in the direction of where the car had been parked.

'In fact,' Sarah continued, because this seemed as good a time as any to start talking about where they went from here, 'I think we need to have a little chat later.'

They had eased themselves out of the crowds now, and Raoul gently deposited Oliver on the ground. He had managed to win a stuffed toy at one of the stalls, and its furry head poked out from the top of his backpack. Insistent on having 'just one more ride', his attention was easily diverted at the promise of the chocolate cake which Raoul told him was waiting in the wicker basket.

'There's a lot to discuss now that the house has been bought. We have to talk about arrangements. I want to get my life in order and really start living it.'

'"Really start living it"?' Raoul's voice had become several shades cooler, and he kept it low because even though Oliver had yanked the stuffed panda out of his backpack and was currently engaged in conversation with it, he was fully aware that careless words could be picked up.

'Well, you have to admit that we've both been in a kind of hiatus over the past few weeks, and I suppose that might have led you to assume…well, the past few weeks have been peculiar…' Sarah took a deep breath. 'I bet you haven't had this much time off work since you started!' She gave a bright laugh at his juncture, although Raoul didn't seem amused. 'It's time for us *both* to come back down to reality…'

They were at the car, and Raoul began hauling stuff out of the boot. Having parked away from the main car park, they found themselves in a private enclosed spot, with shady overhanging trees that seemed designed to indulge prospective picnickers.

His mood had nosedived, although he was at pains not to let Oliver have any inkling of that. He unpacked a quantity of food sufficient to feed a small army, and stuck the chilled wine in the ice bucket which had thoughtfully been provided.

Oblivious of the atmosphere, Oliver attacked the picnic with enthusiasm, and awkward silences were papered over with his chatter as he relived every experience of every ride and tried his best to elicit promises of a return visit.

So she wanted to get back to the land of the living? Why shouldn't she? She was still young, and already she was changing as the worry eased off her shoulders. When he had bumped into her again she had been cleaning floors, and the stress of her situation had shown plainly on her face. Now the contours were returning to her body, and her features had lost the gaunt look that had originally caught him off guard. Why *wouldn't* she want to have some kind of fun? Go to clubs? Lead the life most young people her age were leading and which she had had to sidestep because of the responsibility of having to look after a child?

In every single detail it was a situation that should have suited him perfectly. He had left her once with the best of all possible intentions, and he had never deviated from his resolution to steer clear of the murky waters of matrimony. He was not one of those people who had ever thought that despite coming from no family background to speak of, despite a childhood rife with disillusionment and disappointment, he could somehow turn the tide and become a fully paid up member of the happy-ever-after crew. He had always sworn that the one thing he had taken from his experiences would be his freedom, and although he now had one other person to consider, he certainly wasn't going to go the whole hog and do anything that he would regret. If you only lived life for yourself, no one else had the power to disappoint. It was a credo in which he fully believed.

Okay, so he was still attracted to her. Yes, he hadn't had so many cold showers late at night in his life before. And, sure, she was attracted to him—whether she wanted to believe it of herself or not. But that surely wasn't enough to justify the rising tide of outrage at the thought of her *getting out there*.

Above all else he was practical, and taking this sizzling sexual attraction one step further would just add further complications to an already complicated situation. In fact he should be *urging* her to get out there and live a little. He should be heartily *agreeing* that the very thing they need to do now was plot a clear line forward and get on with it.

Within the next few days he anticipated that Oliver would be told by them, jointly, that he was his father. At that point the domestic bubble which they had built around themselves for a very essential purpose would no longer be required. She was one hundred percent right on that score. Gradually Oliver would come to accept the mundane business of joint custody. It wasn't ideal, but what in life ever really was?

Except he was finding it hard to accept any of those things.

There was a distinct chill in the air as the picnic was cleared away, and on the drive back Oliver, exhausted, fell into a soft sleep. To curtail any opportunity for Sarah to embark on another lengthy exposé of what she intended to do with her free time, Raoul switched on the radio, and the drive was completed in utter silence save for the background noise of middle-of-the-road music.

Twenty minutes from home, Sarah began chatting nervously. Anything to break the silence that was stretching like a piece of tautly pulled elastic between them.

The day which had commenced so wonderfully had ended on a sour note, and the blame for that rested firmly on her shoulders. But the realisation that she had been sliding inexorably back to a very dangerous place—one which she had stupidly occupied five years ago—had made her see the urgency of making sure that her barriers were up and functioning. She would never have believed it possible that time with Raoul could lower her defences to such an extent, but then he had always had a way of stealing into her heart and soul and just somehow *taking over*.

There were some things that she wanted to do to the house as soon as contracts had been exchanged. She wanted to do something lovely and fairly colourful to the walls. So she heard herself chattering inanely about paints and wallpaper while Oliver continued to doze in the back and Raoul continued to stare fixedly at the road ahead, only answering when it would have been ridiculously rude not to.

'Okay,' Sarah said finally, bored by the sound of her own voice droning on about a subject in which he clearly had next to no interest. 'I'm sorry if you think I wrecked the day out.'

'Have I said anything of the sort?'

'You don't have to. It's enough for you to sit there in silence and leave me to do all the talking.'

'You were talking about paint colours and wallpapers. I can't even pretend to manufacture an interest in that. I've already told you that I'll get someone in to do it all. Paint. Wallpaper. Furniture. Hell, I'll even commission someone to buy the art to hang on the walls!'

'Then it wouldn't be a home, would it? I mean, Raoul, have you ever really looked around your apartment?'

'What's that supposed to mean?'

'You have the best of everything that money can buy and it *still* doesn't feel like a home. It's like something you'd see in a magazine! The kitchen looks as though it's never been used, and the sofas look as though they've never been sat on. The rugs look as though nothing's ever been spilled on them. And all that abstract art! I bet you didn't choose a single painting yourself!'

Anger returned her to territory with which she was familiar. The hard, chiselled profile he offered her was expressionless, which made her even angrier. How could she not get to him when he got to her so easily? It wasn't fair!

'I don't *like* abstract art,' she told him nastily. 'In fact I hate it. I like boring, old-fashioned paintings. I like seeing stuff that I can recognise. I like flowers and scenery. I don't enjoying looking at angry lines splashed on a canvas. I can't think of anything worse than some stranger buying art for me because it's going to appreciate. And, furthermore, I don't like leather sofas either. They're cold in winter and hot and sticky in summer. I like warm colours, and soft, squashy chairs you can sink into with a book.'

'I'm getting the picture.' Raoul's mouth was compressed. 'You don't want help when it comes to interior design and you hate my apartment.'

Not given to being unkind, Sarah felt a wave of shame and embarrassment wash over her. She would never normally have dreamt of criticising anyone on their choice of décor for their home. Everyone's taste was different, after all. But the strain of having Raoul around, of enjoying his company and getting a tantalising glimpse of what life could have been had he only wanted and loved her, was finally coming home to roost. For all his moods

and failings, and despite his arrogance, his perverse stub-
bornness and his infuriating ability to be blinkered when
it suited him, he was still one hell of a guy—and this time
round she was seeing so many more sides to him, having
so many more opportunities to tumble straight back into
love.

'*And* we still have to talk,' she said eventually, but con-
tented herself with staring through the window.

If she had hoped to spark a response from him then she
had been sorely mistaken, she thought sourly. Because he
just didn't care one way or another what opinions she had
about him, his apartment, or any other area of his life.

'Yes. We do.'

In an unprecedented move Raoul had done a complete
U-turn. Thinking about her with some other man—point-
lessly projecting, in other words—had been a real turn-
off, and even more annoying had been the fact that he just
hadn't been able to get his thoughts in order. Cool logic
had for once been at odds with an irritating, restless unease which he had found difficult to deal with.

But her little bout of anger and her petulant criticisms
had clarified things in his head, strangely enough.

Sarah wasn't like all the other women he knew, and it
went beyond the fact that she had had his child.

It had always been easy for him to slot the *other* women
who had come and gone like ships passing in the night into
neat, tidy boxes. They'd filled a very clearly defined role
and there were no blurry areas to deal with.

Yes, Sarah had re-entered his life, with a hand grenade
in the form of a child, but only now was he accepting
that her role in his life was riddled with blurry areas. He
didn't know why. Perhaps it was because she represented
a stage in his life before he had made it big and could do
whatever he liked. Or maybe it was just because she was

so damned open, honest and vibrant that she demanded him to engage far more than he was naturally inclined to. She didn't tiptoe around him, and she didn't make any attempts to edit her personality to please him. The women he had dated in the past had all swooned at their first sight of his apartment, with its rampant displays of wealth. He got the impression that the woman sulking in the seat next to him could have written a book on everything she hated about where he lived, and not only that would gladly have given it to him as a present.

The whole situation between them, in fact, demanded a level of engagement that went way beyond the sort of interaction he was accustomed to having with other women. Picnics? Home cooked meals? Board games? *Way* beyond.

He pulled up outside her house, where for once there was a parking space available. Oliver was rousing slowly from sleep, rubbing his eyes and curling into Sarah's arms. Taking the key from her, Raoul unlocked the front door and hesitatingly kissed his son's dark, curly mop of hair. In return he received a sleepy smile.

'He's exhausted,' Sarah muttered. 'All that excitement and then the picnic…he's not accustomed to eating so late. I'll just give him a quick bath and then I think he'll be ready for bed.'

She drew in a deep, steadying breath and firmly trod on the temptation to regret the fact that she had lashed out at him, ruined the atmosphere between them, injected a note of jarring disharmony that made her miserable.

'Why don't you pour yourself something to drink?' she continued, with more command in her voice that she felt. 'And when I come down, like I said, we'll discuss…arrangements.'

She was dishevelled. They had both shared the rides with Oliver, but she had done a few of the really big ones on her own. Someone had had to stay with Oliver, and Raoul had generously offered to babysit, seeing it as a handy excuse to get out of what, frankly, had looked like a terrifying experience. He might have felt sorely deprived as a boy at missing out on all those big rides, but as an adult he could think of nothing worse.

Her hair was tousled and her cheeks were pink, and he noticed the top two buttons of her checked shirt had come undone—although she hadn't yet noticed that.

'Good idea,' he murmured blandly, with a shuttered expression that left her feverishly trying to analyse what he was thinking.

Raoul noted the hectic colour that had seeped into her cheeks, and the way her arms tightened nervously around a very drowsy Oliver. Arrangements certainly needed to be made, he thought. Though possibly not quite along the lines she anticipated.

She wanted to deal with the formalities, and there was no doubt that certain things had to be discussed, but he was running with a different agenda.

At long last he had lost that unsettling, disconcerting feeling that had climbed into the pit of his stomach and refused to budge. He liked having an explanation for everything and he had his explanation now. Sarah was still in his head because she was unfinished business. There were loose ends to their relationship, and he looked forward to tying all those loose ends up and moving on.

He smiled at her slowly, in a way that sent a tingle of maddening sensation running from the tips of her toes to the crown of her head.

'I'll pour you a drink too,' he said, his dark eyes arrowing onto her wary face, taking in the fine bone structure, the wide eyes, the full, eminently kissable mouth. 'And then we can…as you say…begin to talk about moving forward…'

CHAPTER FIVE

SARAH took longer than she had planned. Oliver, for a start, had discovered a new lease of life and demanded his set of toy cars. And Raoul. In that order.

Determined to have a bit of space from wretched Raoul, in which she could clear her head and plan what she was going to say, Sarah had immediately squashed that request and then been forced to compensate for Raoul's absence by feigning absorption in a game of cars which had involved pushing them around the bed in circles, pretending to stop off at key points to refuel.

Forty minutes later she had finally managed to settle him, after which she'd taken herself off for a bath.

She didn't hurry. She felt that she needed all the time she could get to arrange her thoughts.

First things first. She would chat, in a civilised and adult fashion, about the impending necessity to talk to Oliver. She foresaw no problem there.

Secondly she would announce her decision to finally break the news to her parents that Raoul was back on the scene. She would reassure him that there would be no need to meet them.

Thirdly, they were no longer in a relationship—although they were *friends* for Oliver's sake. Just two people with a common link, who had managed to sort out visiting rights without the interference of lawyers because they were both so mature.

She would be at pains to emphasise how *useful* it had been doing stuff together, for the sake of his relationship with his son.

Downstairs, Raoul had removed himself to the sitting room, and Sarah saw, on entering, that he had poured himself a glass of wine. Ever since he had been on the scene her fridge had been stocked with fine-quality wines, and her cheap wine glasses had been replaced with proper ones—expensive, very modern glasses that she would never have dreamt of buying herself for fear of breakages.

He patted the space next to him, which wasn't ideal as far as Sarah was concerned but, given that her only other option was to scuttle to the furthest chair, which would completely ruin the mature approach she was intent on taking, she sat next to him and reached for her drink.

'I think we can say that was a day well spent,' Raoul began, angling his body so that he was directly facing her and crossing his legs, his hand on his thigh loosely holding his glass. 'Despite your rant about the state of my apartment.'

'Sorry about that.' She concentrated hard on sipping her wine.

He shrugged and continued to look at her, his brilliant dark eyes giving very little away. 'Why should you be?'

'I suppose it was a bit rude,' Sarah conceded reluctantly. 'I don't suppose there are very many people who are critical of you...'

'I had no idea you were being critical of *me*. I assumed you were being critical of the décor in my apartment.'

'That's what I meant to say.'

'Because you have to agree that I've taken every piece

of advice you've given and done everything within my power to build connections with Oliver.'

'You've been brilliant,' Sarah admitted. 'Have you… have you enjoyed it? I mean, this whole thing must have turned your world on its head…'

She hadn't actually meant to say that, but it was something they hadn't previously discussed—not in any depth at all. He had accepted the situation and worked with it, but she couldn't help but remember how adamant he had been all those years ago that the last thing he wanted was marriage and children.

'You had your whole life mapped out,' she continued, staring off into the distance. 'You were only a few years older than the rest of us, but you always seemed to know just what you wanted to do and where you wanted to be.'

'Am I sensing some criticism behind that statement?' Raoul harked back to her annoying little summary of the sort of thing she looked for in a man. 'Fun-loving' somehow didn't quite go hand-in-hand with the picture she was painting of him.

'Not really…'

He decided not to pursue this line of conversation, which would get neither of them anywhere fast. 'Good.' He closed the topic with a slashing smile. 'And, to get back to your original question, having Oliver has been an eye-opener. I've never had to tailor my life to accommodate anyone…'

And had he enjoyed it? He hadn't asked himself that question, but thinking about it now—yes, he had. He had enjoyed the curious unpredictability, the small rewards as he began making headway, the first accepting smile that had made his efforts all seem worthwhile…

'If it had been any other kid,' he conceded roughly, 'it would have been a mindless chore, but with Oliver…' He shrugged and let his silence fill in the missing words. 'And, yes, my life had been disrupted. Disrupted in a major way. But there are times when things don't go quite according to plan.'

'Really? I thought that only happened to other people.' Sarah smiled tightly as she remembered all the plans he had made five years ago—none of which had included her. 'What other times have there been in your life when things didn't go according to your plan? In your adult life, I mean? Things don't go according to plan when you let other people into your life, and you've *never* let anyone into your life.'

Okay, so now she was veering madly away from her timetable, but the simmering, helpless resentment she felt after weeks of feeling herself being sucked in by him all over again was conspiring to build to a head. It was as if her mouth had a will of its own and was determined to say stuff her head was telling it not to.

'I mean, just look at your apartment!'

'So we're back to the fact that you don't like chrome, leather and marble…'

'It's more than that!' Sarah cried, frustrated at his polite refusal to indulge her in her histrionics. 'There's nothing personal anywhere in your apartment…'

'You haven't seen all of my apartment,' Raoul pointed out silkily. 'Unless you've been exploring my bedroom when I haven't been looking…'

'No, of course I haven't!' But at that thought she flushed, and shakily took another mouthful of wine.

'Then you shouldn't generalise. I expected better of you.'

'Very funny, Raoul. I'm being serious.'

'And so am I. I've enjoyed spending time with Oliver.

He's my son. Everything he does,' Raoul added, surprising himself with the admission, 'is a source of fascination.'

'You're very good at saying all the right things,' Sarah muttered, half to herself.

Where had her temper tantrum gone? He was refusing to co-operate and now she was reduced to glowering. It took her a few seconds before she brought her mind to bear on the things that needed discussion.

'But I'm really glad that everything is going so well with Oliver, because it brings me to one of the things I want to say.' She cleared her throat and wished that he would stop staring at her like that, with his fabulous eyes half closed and vaguely assessing. 'Oliver has come to like you very much, and to trust you. When he first met you I really thought that it would be a huge uphill struggle for you two to connect. He had no real experience of an adult male in his life, and you had no experience of what to do around young children.'

'Yes, yes, yes. You're not telling me anything I don't already know...'

Sarah's lips tightened and she frowned. She had laid out this conversation in her head and she had already deviated once.

'It's terrific that you haven't seen it all as a chore.'

'If you're hoping to get on my good side, then I should warn you that you're going about it the wrong way. Derogatory remarks about where I live, insinuations that I'm too rigid for parenting...anything else you'd like to throw in the mix before you carry on?'

She thought she detected an undercurrent of amusement in his voice, which made her bristle. 'I think we should both sit down with Oliver and explain the whole situation. I'm not sure if he'll fully take it in, but he's very bright, and I'm hoping that he'll see it as a welcome development.

He's already begun to look forward to your visits.' She
waited. 'Or, of course, I could tell him on my own.'

'No. I like the idea of us doing it together.'

'Good. Well…maybe we should fix a date in the diary?'

'"*Fix a date in the diary*"?' Raoul burst out laughing,
which made Sarah go even redder. 'How formal do we
have to be here?'

'You know what I mean,' she said stiffly. 'You're busy.
I just want to agree on a day.'

'Tomorrow.'

'Fine.'

'Shall I get my phone out so that I can log it in?'

'I'm trying to be serious here, Raoul. After we talk to
Oliver I can talk to my parents. I haven't breathed a word
to them, but Oliver's mentioned you a couple of times when
he's spoken to Mum.'

Nor had she visited her parents in nearly a month. She
was used to nipping down to Devon every couple of weekends, and she was guiltily aware that it had been easier to
fudge and make excuses because her mother would have
been able to eke the truth out of her, and she hadn't wanted
the inevitable sermon.

'But that's not your problem. You won't have to meet
them at all. I'll explain the situation to them…tell them
that we happened to bump into one another… They'll be
pleased because it's always worried them that you were out
there, not knowing that you had fathered a son. I'll have to
explain that I haven't mentioned anything earlier because
I wanted you to get to know Oliver, work through some of
the initial difficulties. I think they'll understand that…'

'And I won't meet them because…?'

'Why should you? You'll be involved in Oliver's life,
but you won't be in mine. Which is really what I want to
talk to you about. Visiting rights and such. I don't think

we have to go through lawyers to work something out, do we? I mean, the past few weeks have been fine. Of course I realise that it's not really been a normal routine for you, but we can work round that. I'm happy to be flexible.'

Raoul found himself recoiling from the deal on the table, even though it was a deal that suited him perfectly. Yes, he had taken a lot of time off work recently. In fact working late into the night, pretty much a routine of his, had been put on temporary hold, and even time catching up in front of his computer had been limited. Her willingness to compromise should have come as a relief. Instead, he was outraged at her easy assumption that he would be fobbed off with a night a week and the occasional weekend as Oliver's confidence levels in him rose.

'Visiting rights...' he repeated, rolling the words on his tongue and not liking how they tasted.

'Yes! You know—maybe an evening a week, whenever suits you. It would be good if you could set aside a specific day, although I know that's probably unrealistic given your lifestyle...'

Quite out of the blue she wondered when his lifestyle outside of work would recommence. His extra-curricular activities. Should she go over old ground? Repeat that she would prefer Oliver not to have to deal with any unfamiliar women? Or would Raoul be sensible enough to understand that without her having to spell it out in black and white?

It was all well and good, laying out these rules and regulations in a calm, sensible voice, but nothing could disguise the sickening thump of her heart when she thought about the longer term. The days when she would wave goodbye to Oliver and watch from the front door of her new house as Raoul sped him away to places and experiences of which she would be ignorant.

She had become accustomed to the threesome.

She had to swallow hard so that the smile on her face didn't falter. 'Aren't you going to say anything?' she prompted uncertainly.

'Let me get this straight,' Raoul intoned flatly. 'We arrange suitable days for me to pick Oliver up and drop him off a couple of hours later, and beyond that our relationship is severed…'

'I'd prefer it if you didn't call it a *relationship*.' She thought of the tingling way he made her feel, and tacking the word *relationship* onto that just seemed to make things worse.

'What would you like me to call it?'

'I'd like to think that we're *friends*. I never thought that I'd see the day when I could refer to you in that way, but I'm pleased to say that I can. Now.'

'Friends…' Raoul murmured.

'Yes. We've really worked well together on this…er… project…' That didn't sound quite right, and she lowered her eyes nervously, realising, with a start that she had managed to drink her glass of wine without even knowing it. She could feel his proximity like a dense, lethal force, and it was all she could do not to squirm away from him.

'And that's what you want, is it, Sarah?'

Dazed and confused, she raised her bright green eyes to his, and was instantly overwhelmed by a feeling of light-headedness.

The sofa was compact. Their knees were almost touching. The last rays of the sun had disappeared into grey twilight, and without benefit of the overhead light his wonderful face was thrown into half shadows.

'Yes, of course,' she heard herself mumble.

'Friends exchanging a few polite words now and again…'

'I think that's how these things go…'

'It's not what I want and you know that.'

A series of disconcerting images flashed through Sarah's mind at indecent speed. All the simple little things they had done together over the past few weeks…things that had shattered her confidence in her ability to keep a respectable distance from him. And now here he was, framing the very words she didn't want to hear.

'Raoul…' she breathed shakily.

Raoul homed in on the hesitancy in her voice with an unassailable feeling of triumph. It had shocked him to realise how much he still wanted her—until he had worked out the whole theory of unfinished business. With that explanation in his head, he could now easily see why he had been finding it difficult to concentrate at work—why images of her kept floating in his mind, like bits of shrapnel in his system, ruining his concentration and his ability to focus.

'I like it when you say my name.' Right now the lack of focus thing seemed to be happening big-time. His voice lacked its usual self assured resonance. He extended his arm along the back of the sofa and then allowed his hand to drop to the back of her neck, where he slowly caressed the soft, smooth skin.

Sarah struggled to remember the very important fact that Raoul Sinclair was a man who was programmed to get exactly what he wanted—except she didn't know why on earth he would want *her*. But she felt her body sag as she battled to bring some cool reasoning to the situation.

Her moss green eyes were welded to his, and the connection was as strong as a bond of steel.

'I really want to kiss you right now.' He sounded as unsteady as she looked.

'No. You don't. You can't. You mustn't…'

'You're not convincing me…'

She knew that he was going to kiss her, just as she knew that she should push him away. But she couldn't move. Her slender body was as still as a statue, although deep inside was a torrential surge of sensation that was already threatening to break through its fragile barriers.

The touch of his mouth against hers was intoxicating, and she fell back, weakened with fierce arousal. With an unerring sensual instinct that was uniquely his Raoul closed the small distance between them. Or maybe her treacherous body had done that of its own sweet accord. Sarah didn't know. She was ablaze with a hungry craving that had been building for weeks. She moaned softly, and then louder as he trailed an exploring hand underneath her top, sending electric shocks through her whole body.

The hand that had flattened against his chest, aiming to push him away, first curled into a useless fist and then splayed open to clutch the neck of his shirt, so that she could pull him towards her.

She was burning up, and her breasts felt tender, her nipples tightening in anticipation. She strove to stifle a shameless groan of pleasure as his hand climbed higher, caressing her ribcage, moving round to unhook her bra.

As sofas went, this sofa was hardly the most luxurious in the world, but Raoul didn't think he could make it up the stairs to her bedroom. He tugged the cotton top over her head, taking her bra with it in the process, and gazed at her, half undressed, her eyes slumbrous, her perfect mouth half parted on a smile while her breasts rose and fell in quick rhythm with her breathing.

He couldn't believe how much he wanted her. Pure, driven sensation wiped out all coherent thought. If the house had suddenly been struck by an earthquake, he wasn't sure he would have noticed.

The effect she had on him was instantaneous, and as he fluidly removed his clothes he marvelled at his incredible sense of recall. It was as if his memories of her had never been buried, as he had imagined, but instead had remained intact, very close to the surface. It proved conclusively that she was the one woman in his life he had never forgotten because what they'd shared had been prematurely concluded. He had never had time to get tired of her.

Sarah watched as his clothes hit the ground. For a businessman he still had the hard, highly toned, muscular body of an athlete. Broad shoulders narrowed to a six pack and...

Her eyes were riveted by the evidence of his impressive arousal.

'You still like looking at me,' Raoul said with a slow smile. 'And I still like you looking at me.'

The touch of her slight hand on his erection drew a shudder from him, and he curled his fingers in her hair as he felt the delicacy of her mouth and tongue take over from where her hand had been.

Sarah, in some dim part of her mind, knew that she should pull back, should tell him that this was now and not then. But she had always been achingly weak around him and nothing had changed.

The taste of him simply transported her. She found that she couldn't think. Everything had narrowed down to this one moment in time. Her body, which had spent the past five years in cold storage, roared into life and there was nothing she could do about it.

She wriggled out of the rest of her clothes.

She was barely aware of him moving to shut the sitting room door, then tossing one of the throws from a chair onto the ground. She *was* aware of him muttering something about the sofa not being a suitable spot for lovemaking for anyone who wasn't vertically challenged.

The fleecy throw was wonderfully soft and thick.

'This is much better,' Raoul growled, straddling her and then leaning down so that he could kiss her. At the same time he slid his hands under her back, so that she was arched up to him, her breasts scraping provocatively against his chest. 'There's no way that a five-foot sofa can accommodate my six foot two inches.'

'I don't recall you being that fussy five years ago,' Sarah said breathlessly. There was so much of him that she wanted to touch, so much that she had missed.

'You'll have to tell me if I've lost my sense of adventure,' he murmured. He felt her twist restlessly under him. It was a cause of deep satisfaction that he knew exactly what she wanted.

He reared back and began to caress her breasts, looking down at her flushed face as he massaged them, rolling his thumbs over the pouting tips of her nipples while she, likewise, attended to his throbbing erection.

This was a foreplay of mutual satisfaction between two people comfortable with each other's wants. It was like resuming the steps to a well-rehearsed dance.

He bent so that he could feather her neck with kisses— soft, tender nibbles that produced little gasps and moans— and then, taking advantage of the breasts offered up to his exploring mouth, he began to suckle the pink crests, drawing one distended nipple into his mouth, driving her crazy, and making her impatient for him to do the same to the other breast.

It was incredible to think that the body he was now touching had carried his child, and a wave of bitter regret washed over him. So the circumstances would have been all wrong, and he had never factored a child into his life plan, but he would have risen to the challenge. He would have been there right from the very start. He wouldn't have missed out on the first four years of his son's life. He wouldn't have been obliged to spend weeks playing catch up in the father stakes.

But regret was not an emotion with which Raoul was accustomed to dealing, and there was no value in looking at things with the benefit of hindsight.

He blocked out the fanciful notion of a different path and instead trailed his mouth over the flat planes of her stomach, maybe not quite so firm as it had once been, but remarkably free of stretch marks.

The taste of her, as he dipped his tongue to tease her most sensitive spot, was the most erotic thing he had ever experienced.

He smoothed his hands over the satin smoothness of her inner thighs and she groaned as he gave his full attention to the task.

Several times he took her so close to the edge that she had to use every ounce of will-power to rein herself back. She wanted him inside her. She found that she was desperate to feel that wonderful moment when he took one deep, final thrust and lost all his control as he came.

'Are you protected?'

Those three words penetrated her bubble, and it took a few seconds for them to register.

'Huh?'

'I haven't got any protection with me.' Raoul's voice was thick with frustration. 'And you're not on the pill. I can tell from the expression on your face.'

'No. I'm not.' It was slowly sinking in that, however wrapped up he was in the throes of passion, there was no way he would permit another mistake to occur. Look at what his last slip-up had cost him!

'Still, there are other ways of pleasing each other...'

'No, I can't... I'm sorry... I don't know what happened...'

She rolled onto her side, feeling exposed, and then sat up and looked around to where their clothes lay in random piles on the ground. Reaching out, she picked up her top and hastily shoved it on. This was followed by her underwear, while Raoul watched in silence, before heaving himself up on one elbow to stare at her with brooding force.

'Don't tell me that you've suddenly decided to have an attack of scruples now!'

'This was a mistake!' She backed away from him to take refuge on the sofa, drawing her knees up and hugging herself to stave off a bad bout of the shakes.

She dragged her eyes away from the powerful image of his nudity. She wished that she could honestly tell herself that she had just given in to a temporary urge that had been too strong. But the questions raining down on her were of an altogether more uncomfortable nature.

How far had she *really* come these past few years? Had she forgotten just how easily he had found it to dump her? To write her off as surplus to requirements when it came to the big plan of how he wanted to live his life?

A few weeks ago Raoul Sinclair had been the biggest mistake she had ever made. Seeing him again had been a shock, but she had risen above that and tried hard to view his reappearance in her life as something good for the sake of Oliver.

Yes, he had still been able to get to her, but her defences had been up and she had been prepared to fight to protect herself.

But he had attacked her in a way she had never planned for. He had won her over with the ease with which he had accepted what must have been a devastating blow to all his long-term plans. He had controlled his ego and his pride to listen to what she had to say, and he had thrown himself into the business of getting to know his son with enthusiasm and heart wrenching humility. Against her will, and against all logic and reason and good judgement, she had succumbed over the weeks to his sense of humour, his patience with Oliver, his determination to go the extra mile.

How many men who had never contemplated having a family, indeed had steadfastly maintained their determination never to go down that road, would have reacted to similar news with the grace that he had?

Sarah suspected that a lot would either have walked away or else would have contributed financially but done the absolute minimum beyond that.

He had reminded her of all the reasons she had fallen in love with him in the first place and more.

Was it any wonder that she had been a sitting target when he had reached out and touched her?

Sarah could have wept, because she knew that fundamentally Raoul hadn't changed. He might want her body, but he didn't want her dreams, her hopes or her romantic notions—which, it now seemed, had never abandoned her after all, because they were part and parcel of who she was.

'Of course this wasn't a mistake!' He raked impatient fingers through his hair and looked at her as he got dressed. Huddled on the sofa in front of him she looked very young—but then, of course, she *was* very young. Had he presumed too much? No. Of course he hadn't. Her signals had been loud and clear. She had given him the green light, and for the life of him he couldn't understand why she was backing away from him now. The past few weeks had been inexorably leading to this place. At least that was how he saw it.

It wasn't just that she still had the same dramatic eff

on his libido that she'd always had. It wasn't just that she could look at him from under those feathery lashes and make him break out in a sweat. No, they had connected in a much more fundamental area, and he knew that she felt the same way. Hell, he was nothing if not brilliant when it came to reading the signs.

And just then? Before she had decided to start back-tracking? She had been as turned on as him!

'In fact,' he said huskily, 'it was the most natural thing in the world.'

'How do you figure that?'

'You're the mother of my child. I happen to think that it's pretty damned good that we're still seriously attracted to one another.' He sat on the sofa, elbows on thighs, and looked sideways at her.

'Well, I don't think it's good. I think it just…complicates everything.'

'How does it complicate everything?'

'I don't want to get into a relationship with you. Oh, God—I forgot you don't like the word *relationship*. I forgot you find it too threatening.'

Raoul could feel her trying to impose a barrier between them and he didn't like it. It annoyed him that she was prepared to waste time dwelling on something as insignificant as a simple word.

'I want you to admit what's obvious,' he told her, turning so that he was facing her directly, not giving her the slightest opportunity to deflect her eyes from his. 'You can't deny the sexual chemistry between us. If anything, it's stronger than it was when we were together five years ago.'

It terrified Sarah that he felt that too—that it hadn't been just a trick of her imagination that she was drawn to him on all sorts of unwelcome and unexpected levels. In

Africa they had come together as two young people about to take their first steps into the big, bad world. They had lived in a bubble, far removed from day-to-day life. There was no bubble here, and that made the savage attraction she felt for him all the more terrifying.

'No...' she protested weakly.

'Are you telling me that if I hadn't interrupted our love-making you would have suddenly decided to push me away?'

Sarah went bright red and didn't say anything.

'I thought so,' Raoul confirmed softly. 'You want to push me away but you can't.'

'Don't tell me what I can and can't do.'

'Okay. Well, let me tell you this. The past few weeks have been...a revelation. Who would have thought that I could enjoy spending so much time in a kitchen? Especially a kitchen with no mod-cons? Or sitting in front of a television watching a children's programme? I never expected to see you again, but the second I did I realised that what I felt for you hadn't gone away as I had assumed it had. I still want you, and I'm not too proud to admit it.'

'Wanting someone isn't enough...' But her words were distinctly lacking in conviction.

'It's a damn sight healthier than self-denial.' Raoul let those words settle. 'Martyrs might feel virtuous, but virtue is a questionable trade off when it goes hand in hand with unhappiness.'

'You are just *so* egotistical!' Sarah said hotly. 'Are you really saying that I'm going to be unhappy if I pass up the fantastic opportunity to sleep with you?'

'You're going to be miserable if you pass up the opportunity to put this thing we have to bed. You keep trying to deny it. You blow hot and cold because you want to kid yourself that you can fight it.'

Sarah would have liked to deny that, but how could she? He was right. She wavered between wanting him to touch her, enjoying it madly when he did, and being repelled by her own lack of will-power.

'I don't like thinking of you going to clubs and meeting guys,' he admitted roughly.

'Why? Would you be jealous?'

'How can I be jealous of what, as yet, doesn't even exist? Besides, jealousy isn't my thing.' He lowered his eyes and shifted. 'You still have a hold over me,' he conceded. 'I still want you...'

'There's more to life than the physical stuff,' Sarah muttered under her breath.

'Let's agree to differ on that score,' Raoul contradicted without hesitation. 'And it doesn't change the fact that we're going to end up in bed sooner rather than later. I'm proposing we make it sooner. We're unfinished business, Sarah...'

'What do you mean?'

Raoul took her fingers and played with them idly, keeping his eyes locked to hers. 'Back then, I did what was right for both of us. But would what we had have ended had it not been for the fact that I was due to leave the country?'

'Yes, it *would* have ended, Raoul. Because you're not interested in long-term relationships. Oh, we might have drifted on for a few more months, but sooner or later you would have become tired of me.'

'Sooner or later you would have discovered that you were pregnant,' Raoul pointed out with infuriating calm.

'And how would that have changed anything? Of course it wouldn't! You would have stuck around for the baby because you have a sense of responsibility, but why don't you admit that there's no way we would have ended up together!'

'How do I know what would have happened? Do I have a crystal ball?'

'You don't need a crystal ball, Raoul. You just need to be honest. If we had continued our…our whatever you want to call it…would it have led to marriage? Some kind of commitment? Or would we have just carried on sleeping together until the business between us was finally finished? In other words, until you were ready to move on? I know I'm sometimes weak when I'm around you. You're an attractive guy, and you also happen to be the father of my child. But that doesn't mean that it would be a good idea to just have lots of sex until you get me out of your system…'

'What makes you think that it wouldn't be the other way around?'

'In fact,' she continued, ignoring his interruption, 'it would be selfish of us to become lovers because we're incapable of a bit of self-denial! I don't want Oliver to become so accustomed to you being around that it's a problem when you decide to take off! I'm sorry I've given you mixed signals, but we're better off just being…friends…'

CHAPTER SIX

SARAH wondered how she had managed to let her emotions derail her to such an extent that she had nearly ended up back in bed with Raoul. The words *unfinished business* rankled, conjuring up as they did visions of something disposable, to be picked up and then discarded once again the minute it suited him.

Had he imagined that she would launch herself into his arms in a bid to take up where they had left off? Had he thought that she would greet his assertion about still wanting her as something wonderful and complimentary? He didn't want her seeing anyone else—not because he wanted to work on having a proper relationship with her, but because he wanted her to fill his bed until such time as he managed to get her out of his system. Like a flu virus.

He was an arrogant, selfish bastard, and she had been a crazy fool to get herself lulled into thinking otherwise!

She had a couple of days' respite, because he was out of the country, and although he telephoned on both days she was brief before passing him over to Oliver, which he must have found extra challenging, given Oliver's long silences and excitable babbling.

'I think we'll tell him at the weekend,' she informed Raoul crisply, and politely told him that there would be absolutely no need for him to rush over the second he got back, because at that time of night Oliver would be asleep anyway.

On the other side of the Atlantic, Raoul scowled down the phone. He should never have let her think about what he had said. He should have kissed her doubts away and then just made love to her until she was silenced.

Except, of course, she would still have jumped on her moral bandwagon. What had been so straightforward for him had been a hotbed of dilemma for her. He told himself that there were plenty of other fish in the sea, but when he opened his address book and started scanning down the names of beautiful women, all of whom would have shrieked with joy at the sound of his voice and the prospect of a hot date, he found his enthusiasm for that kind of replacement therapy waning fast.

Whereas before he had been comfortable turning up at Sarah's without much notice, he had now found himself given a very definite time slot, and so he arrived at her house bang on five-thirty to find Oliver dressed in jeans and a jumper while she was in her oldest clothes, her hair wet from the shower and pinned up into a ponytail.

'I thought we could sit him down and explain the situation to him,' were her opening words, 'and then you could take him out for something to eat. Nothing fancy, but it'll be nice for him to have you to himself without me around. I've also explained the whole situation to Mum and Dad. They're very pleased that you're on the scene.'

Within minutes Raoul had got the measure of what was going on. She was making it perfectly clear that they would now be communicating on a need-to-know basis only. Her bright green eyes were guarded and detached, only warming when they had Oliver between them so that they could explain the situation.

Finally fatherhood was fully conferred onto him. He was no longer the outsider, easing himself in. He was a dad, and as she had predicted it was a smooth transfer. Oliver had had time to adjust to him. He accepted the news with solemnity, and then it was as though nothing had changed. Raoul had brought him back a very fancy but admirably small box of bricks and an enormous paint-box, both of which were greeted with enthusiasm.

'Take a few pictures when he starts painting in your living room,' Sarah said sarcastically. 'I'd love to see how your leather furniture reacts to the watercolours.'

'Is this how it's now going to be?' Raoul enquired coldly, as Oliver stuffed his backpack with lots of unnecessary items in preparation for their meal out.

Defiant pink colour suffused Sarah's cheeks. She didn't want to be argumentative. He was going to be on the scene, in one way or another, for time immemorial, and she knew that they had to develop a civil, courteous relationship if they weren't to descend into a parody of two warring parents. But she was truly scared of reaching the point they previously had, which had been one of such easy friendship that all the feelings she had imagined left behind had found fertile ground and blossomed out of control. She had let him crawl under her skin until the only person she could think about had been him, so that when he'd finally touched her she had gone up in flames.

'No. It's not. I apologise for that remark,' she responded stiffly, stooping down to adjust Oliver's backpack, whilst taking the opportunity to secretly remove some of the unnecessary stuff he had slipped in. 'Now, you're going to be a good boy, Oliver, aren't you? With your dad?' Oliver nodded and Sarah straightened back up to address Raoul. 'What time can I expect you back? Because I'm going out. I'll only be a couple of hours.'

'You're going out? Where?'

Raoul gave her the once-over. Sloppy clothes. Damp hair. She was waiting for them to leave before she got dressed.

'I don't think that's any of your business, actually.'

'And what if you're not back when I return?'

'You have my mobile number, Raoul. You could always give me a call.'

'Who are you going to be with?'

Raoul knew that it was an outrageous question. He thought back to his brief—very brief—notion that he might get in touch with another woman, go on a date. The idea had lasted less than ten seconds. So...who was *she* going out with? On the first evening he had Oliver? With a man? What man? She had claimed that there was no one at all in her life, that she had been just too busy with the business of trying to earn some money and be a single parent. She might not have had the time to cultivate any kind of personal life, but that didn't mean that there hadn't been men hovering on the periphery, ready to move in just as soon as she found the time.

The more Raoul thought about it, the more convinced he became that she was meeting a man. One of those sensitive, fun-loving types she professed to like. Had she made sure to appear in old clothes so that he wouldn't be able to gauge where she was going by what she was wearing?

He was the least fanciful man in the world, and yet he couldn't stop the swirl of wildly imaginative conclusions to which he was jumping. He was tempted to stand his ground until he got answers that satisfied him.

Sarah laughed incredulously at his question. 'I can't believe you just asked that, Raoul.'

'Why?'

'Because it's none of your business. Now, Oliver's beginning to get restless.' She glanced down to where he was beginning to fidget, delivering soft taps to the skirting board with his shoe and tugging Raoul's hand impatiently. 'I'll see you in a couple of hours, and you know how to get hold of me if you need to.'

Sarah thought that it was a damning indication of just how quickly their relationship had slipped back into dangerous waters—the fact that he saw it as his right to know what she was getting up to. They might not have become lovers, the way they once had been, but it had been a close call. Had she sent out signals? Without even being aware of doing so?

She was going out with a girlfriend for a pizza. Wild horses wouldn't have dragged the admission out of her. She would be gone an hour and a half, tops, and whilst she knew that she shouldn't care one way or another if he knew that her evening out was a harmless bit of catching up with a pal, she did.

So instead of her jeans she wore a mini-skirt, and instead of her trainers she wore heels. She wasn't quite sure what she was trying to prove, and she certainly felt conspicuous in the pizza parlour, where the dress code was more dressing down than dressing up, but she was perversely pleased that she had gone to the trouble when she opened the door to Raoul two and a half hours later.

Oliver was considerably less pristine than he had been when he had left. In fact, Sarah thought that she could pretty much guess at what they had eaten for dinner from the various smears on his clothes.

'How did it go?'

Raoul had to force himself to focus on what she was asking, because the sight of her tight short skirt and high black heels were threatening to ambush his thinking processes.

'Very well…' He heard himself going through the motions of polite chit-chat, bending down to ruffle Oliver's hair and draw him into the conversation. Crayons and paper had been produced at the restaurant, and he had drawn some pictures. Happy family stuff. There would be a psychologist somewhere who would be able to say something about the stick figure drawings of two parents and a child in the middle.

'Right… Well…'

Raoul frowned as she began shutting the door on him. He inserted himself into the small hallway.

'We need to discuss the details of this arrangement,' he told her smoothly. 'As well as the details of the house move. Everything's signed. I'll need to know what needs to be removed from this place.'

'Already?'

'Time moves on at a pace, doesn't it?'

Sarah fell back and watched him stride towards the sitting room. 'I'll get Oliver to bed and be back down in a sec,' she mumbled helplessly to his departing back.

Tempted to get out of her ridiculous gear, she decided against it. Whatever technicalities had to be discussed wouldn't take long, although she was surprised at how fast the house had become available. The last time she had seen it, it had been something of a derelict shell. At the time, she had confided in Raoul what she would like in terms of furniture, but that was the last she had heard on the subject, which had been a couple of weeks ago. She had assumed that the whole process would take months, and had deferred thinking about the move until it was more imminent.

'I can't believe the house is ready. Are you sure?' This as soon as she was back in the sitting room, where he was relaxed in one of the chairs, with his back to the bay window. 'I thought these things took months…'

'Amazing what money can do when it comes to speeding things up.'

'But I haven't really thought about what to fill it with. I mean, none of this stuff is mine…'

'Which is a blessing, judging from the quality of the furnishings.' Raoul watched as she nervously took the chair facing his on the opposite side of the tiny sitting room. She had to wriggle the short skirt down so that it didn't indecently expose her thighs and his lips thinned disapprovingly. The top was hardly better. A vest affair that contoured her generous breasts in a way that couldn't fail to arouse interest.

Sarah couldn't be bothered to react because she didn't disagree.

'It's going to be weird leaving here,' she thought out loud.

'Oliver's excited.' *Who had the short skirt and the tight top and the high heels been for?* 'He's looking forward to having a bigger garden. Complete with the swing set I promised him. Did you enjoy your evening?'

Sarah, who had still been contemplating the prospect of being uprooted sooner than she had expected, looked at Raoul in sudden confusion.

'You're dressed like a tart,' he expanded coolly, 'and I don't like it.'

Sarah gripped the arms of the chair while a slow burning anger rose inside her like red spreading mist.

'How *dare* you think that you can tell me how I can dress?'

'You never wore clothes like that when I was around. Yet the very first time you have a bit of free time without Oliver you're dressed to the nines. I'm guessing that you've used your time profitably by checking what's out there for a single girl.'

'I don't have to…to…*dignify* that with a response!'

No, she didn't, and her stubborn, glaring eyes were telling him that he was going to get nowhere when it came to dragging an explanation of her whereabouts out of her.

Hot on the heels of her rejection, her self-righteous proclamation that their sleeping together wasn't going to be on the cards, her strident reminders to him that she wanted commitment, Raoul finally acknowledged what had been staring him in the face.

When it came to Sarah he was possessive, and he wanted exclusivity. He didn't want her dipping her toe into the world of dating and other men. Seeing her in that revealing get-up, he realised that he didn't even want her dressing in a way that could conceivably attract them. If she had to wear next to nothing, then he wanted it to be for his benefit and his benefit only.

He had never been possessive in his life before. Was it because she was more than just a woman to him? Because she was the mother of his child? Did he have some peculiar dinosaur streak of which he had hitherto been unaware? He just knew that the thought of her trawling the clubs made his blood run cold.

So he had never been moved by the notion of settling down with anyone? Well, life wasn't a static business. Rules and guidelines made yesterday became null and void when situations changed. Wasn't flexibility a sign of a creative mind?

He wondered that he could have been disingenuous enough to imagine his perfectly reasonable proposition that they take what they had and run with it might be met with enthusiasm. Sarah would never settle for anything less than a full-time relationship. And would that even be with him? he wondered uneasily. It was true that the sexual chemistry between them was electrifying, but it certainly wouldn't be the tipping point for her.

'Let's just talk about the practicalities,' she continued firmly. 'If you give me a definite date as to when we need to be out of here... I haven't given notice to the landlord,' she said suddenly. 'I need to give three months' notice...'

'I'll take care of that.'

'And I suppose we should discuss what days suit you to come and see Oliver. Or should we wait until we're settled in the new place? Then you can see how easy it is for you to get to where we are. Public transport can be a little un-reliable. Oops, sorry—I forgot that you wouldn't be tak-ing public transport...'

Raoul was acidly wondering whether she was eager to get her diary in order, so that she knew in advance when she would be able to slot in her exciting single life. What the hell was going on here? He was *jealous*!

He stood up, and Sarah hastily followed suit, bemused by the fact that he seemed to be leaving pretty much as fast as he had arrived. Not only that, but he had somehow managed to make her feel like a cheap tart. Although she knew that he had no right to pass sweeping judgements on what she wore or where she went, she still had to fight the temptation to make peace by just telling him the truth.

'The house will be ready by the middle of next week.'

'But what about my things?'

'I'll arrange to have them brought over. If all this fur-niture is staying, then I can't imagine that what's left will amount to much.'

'No, I suppose not,' she said in a small voice, perversely inclined to dither now that he was on his way out.

Raoul hesitated. 'It's going to be fine,' he said roughly.

'The house will be entirely in your name. You won't have to be afraid that you could lose the roof over your head, and really, it's just a change of location.'

'It'll be great!' She tried a bright smile on for size. 'I know Mum and Dad are really thrilled about it. They haven't been too impressed with our rented house, what with the busy street so close to the front door and not much back garden for Oliver.'

'Which brings me to something I haven't yet mentioned. Your parents.'

'What about them?'

'I want to meet them.'

'Whatever for?' Sarah asked, dismayed. Try as she had, she couldn't stop feeling deeply suspicious that neither of them had really believed her when she had told them that Raoul was back on the scene but that it was absolutely fine because she had discovered that she felt nothing for him.

'Because Oliver's my son and it makes sense for me to know his grandparents. There will be occasions when they visit us in London and vice versa.'

'Yes, but…'

'I also don't want to spend the rest of my life with your parents harbouring misconceptions about the kind of man I am.'

'They don't have misconceptions,' Sarah admitted grudgingly. 'I told them how much time you'd spent with Oliver, and also about the house.'

'I'd still like to meet them, so you'll have to arrange that and give me a few days' advance notice.'

'Well, maybe when they're next in London…'

'No. Maybe within the next fortnight.'

With the house move a heartbeat away, and a date set in the diary for the three of them to visit her parents in

Devon, Sarah had never felt more like someone chucked onto a rollercoaster and managing to hang on only by the skin of her teeth.

Her possessions, once she had packed them all up, amounted to a few cardboard boxes, which seemed a sad indictment of the time she had spent in the rented house. Nor could she say, with her hand on her heart, that there was very much that she would miss about where she'd lived. The neighbours were pleasant enough, although she knew them only in passing, but the place was wrapped up in so many memories of hardship and trying to make ends meet that she found herself barely glancing back as the chauffeur-driven car that had been sent for them arrived to collect her promptly on Wednesday morning.

Oliver could barely contain his excitement. The back of the opulent car was strewn with his toys. Of course Raoul's driver knew who they were, because from the start Raoul had flatly informed her that he couldn't care less what other people thought of his private life, but she could see that the man was curious, and amused at Oliver's high spirits. Sarah wondered whether he was trying to marry the image of his boss with that of a man who wouldn't mind a four-year-old child treating his mega-expensive car with cavalier disrespect.

Sarah was charmed afresh at the peaceful, tree-lined road that led up to the house, which was in a large corner plot. Anyone could have been forgiven for thinking that London was a million miles away. It was as far removed from their small rented terraced house on the busy road as chalk was from cheese. Whatever her doubts and anxieties, she couldn't deny that Raoul had rescued them both from a great deal of financial hardship and discomfort.

Hard on the heels of that private admission she felt a

lump in her throat at the thought of them being *friends*. She had been so offended by his suggestion that they become lovers for no other reason than they were still attracted to one another, and so hurt that he only wanted her in his bed as a way of exorcising old ghosts... She had positively done the right thing in telling him just where he could take that selfish, arrogant proposal, and yet...

Had she reacted too hastily?

Sarah hurriedly sidelined that sign of weakness and scooped Oliver's toys onto her lap as the car finally slowed down and then swept up the picturesque drive to the house.

Raoul was waiting for her inside.

'I would have brought you here,' he said, picking up Oliver, who demanded to be put down so that he could explore, 'but I've come straight from work.'

'That's okay.' Sarah stepped inside and her mouth fell open—because it bore little resemblance to the house she had last seen.

Flagstone tiles made the hallway warm and colourful, and everywhere else rich, deep wood lent a rustic, cosy charm. She walked from room to room, taking in the décor which was exactly as she would have wanted it to be, from the velvet drapes in the sitting room to the restored Victorian tiles around the fireplace.

Raoul made a show of pointing out the bottle-green Aga which took pride of place in the kitchen, and the old-fashioned dresser which he had had specifically sourced from one of the house magazines which had littered her house.

'You had a crease in the page,' he informed her, 'so I took it to mean that this was the kind of thing you liked.'

Oliver had positioned himself by the French doors that led from the small conservatory by the kitchen into the

garden, and was staring at the swing set outside with eyes
as round as saucers.

'Okay,' Sarah said on a laugh, holding his hand, 'let's
have a look outside, shall we?'

'I don't remember the garden being this well planted,'
she said, looking around her at the shrubs and foliage that
framed the long lawn. There was even a rustic table and
chairs on the paved patio, behind which a trellis promised
a riot of colour when in season.

'I had it landscaped. Feel free to change anything you
want. Why don't we have a look upstairs? I can get my
driver to keep an eye on Oliver,' he added drily. 'We might
have a fight on our hands if we try and prise him off the
swing.'

Raoul had had considerable input with the furnishings.
He had hired the very same mega-expensive interior designer who had done his own penthouse apartment, but
instead of handing over an enormous cheque and giving
her free rein he had actually been specific about what
he wanted. He knew that Sarah hated anything modern
and minimalist. He'd steered clear of anything involving
leather and chrome. He had stopped short of buying artwork, although he had been tempted by some small land-
scapes that would have been a terrific investment, but he
had done his utmost with a bewildering range of colour
options and had insisted that everything be kept period.

'I can't believe this is going to be our new home,' Sarah
murmured yet again, as she ran her hands lovingly over
the Victorian fireplace in what would be her bedroom.
A dreamy four-poster bed dominated the space, and the
leaded windows overlooked the pretty garden. She could
see Oliver on the swing, being pushed by Raoul's very patient driver, and she waved at him.

'Did you choose all this stuff yourself?'

Raoul flushed. How cool was it to have a hand in choosing furnishings for a house? Not very. Especially when there had been a million and one other things clamouring for his attention at work. But he had been rattled by her rejection, and had realised that despite what he saw as an obvious way forward for them he could take nothing for granted.

'I think I know what you like,' he prevaricated, and received a warm smile in response.

Sarah squashed the temptation to hug him. He did things like this and was it any wonder that her will-power was all over the place? She had expected to find a house that was functioning and kitted out in a fairly basic way. Instead there was nothing that wasn't one hundred percent perfect, from the mellow velvet curtains in the sitting room to the faded elegant wallpaper in the bedroom.

Oliver's room, next to hers, was what any four-year-old boy would have dreamt of, with a bed in the shape of a racing car and wallpaper featuring all his favourite cartoon characters.

Yet again she had to remind herself that she had done the right thing in turning her back on what had been on offer. Yet again she forced herself back onto the straight and narrow by telling herself that, however good Raoul was at being charming, going the extra mile and throwing money at something with a generosity that would render most people speechless, he was still a man who walked alone and always would. He was still a man with an in-built loathing of any form of commitment, which in his head was the equivalent of a prison sentence.

Yet again she was forced to concede that his invitation to be his lover would have sounded the death knell for any ongoing amicable relationship they might foster, because she would have been the one to get hurt in the end. She knew that if she got too close to him it would be impossible to hold any of herself back.

But the steps he had taken to ensure that she walked into a house that was brilliant in every way moved her.

'We'll have to sit down and talk about visiting.' She strived to hit the right note of being convivial, appreciative but practical.

Raoul looked at her with veiled eyes. Had he hoped for a more favourable reaction, given the time and effort he had expended in doing this house up for her? Since when did *quid pro quo* play a part in human interaction? Was this the legacy that had been willed to him courtesy of his disadvantaged background?

He thrust aside that moment of introspection, but even so he knew that she was sliding further and further away from him.

'I don't want to have weekly visits,' he told her, lounging on the ledge by the window and surveying her with his arms folded.

'No...well, you can come as often as you like,' she offered. 'I just really would need to find out exactly when, so that Oliver isn't disappointed...I know your work life makes you unpredictable...'

'Have I been unpredictable so far?'

'No, but...'

'I've come every time I said I would. Believe me, I understand how important it is to be reliable when there's a child involved. You forget I have intimate experience of kids waiting by windows with their bags packed for parents who never showed up.'

'Of course...'

'I know how damaging that can be.'

'So...what do you suggest? He'll be starting school in September...maybe weekends might be a good idea. Just to begin with. Until he gets used to his new routine. Kids can be tetchy and exhausted when they first start school…'

'I'm not in favour of being a part-time father.'

'You *won't* be.'

'How am I to know that would be a continuing state of affairs?'

'I don't understand…'

'How long before you find another man, in other words?' He thought of her, dressed to kill, on the hunt for a soulmate.

Sarah stared at him incredulously. Slowly the nuts and bolts cranked into gear and she gave a shaky, sheepish laugh. 'Okay. I know what you're getting at. You think that I went somewhere exciting the last time you took Oliver out. You think that I got dressed up and decided to…I don't know…paint the town red…'

Raoul flushed darkly and kept his eyes pinned to her face.

'Do you really think that I'm the type of person who keeps her head down, bringing up a child, and then hits the clubs the very second she gets a couple of hours out of the house?'

'It's not that impossible to believe. Don't forget you were the one who made a big song and dance about wanting to be free to find your knight in shining armour! If such a person exists!'

'Oh, for heaven's sake!' She walked towards him, angry, frustrated, and helplessly aware that the only contender for the vacancy of knight in shining armour was standing right in front of her—the very last man on whom the honour should ever be conferred because he wasn't interested in the position. 'Look, I didn't go *anywhere* last Saturday. Well, nowhere exciting at any rate. I met my friend and we went out for a pizza. Are you satisfied?'

'What friend was this?'

'A girlfriend from Devon. She moved to London a few months ago, and we try to get together as often as we can. It's not always possible with a young child, and so I took advantage of having a night off to have dinner with her.'

'Why didn't you tell me at the time?'

'Because it was none of your business, Raoul!'

'Did it give you a kick to make me jealous?'

It was the first time he had ever expressed an emotion like that. Many times he had told her that he just wasn't a jealous person. His admission now brought a rush of heady colour to her cheeks, and she could feel her heart accelerate, beating against her ribcage like a sledgehammer. Suddenly conscious of his proximity, she widened her eyes and heard her breaths come fast and shallow. She feverishly tried to work out what this meant. Did he feel more for her than he had been willing to verbalise? Or was she just caving in once again? Clutching at straws because she loved him?

'You're telling me that you were *jealous*?'

Having said more than he had intended to, Raoul refused to be drawn into a touchy feely conversation about a passing weakness. He looked at her with stubborn pride.

'I'm telling you that I wasn't impressed by the way you were dressed.' He heard himself expressing an opinion that would have been more appropriate had it come from someone three times his age. 'You're a mother…'

'And so short skirts are out? I'm *not* getting all wrapped up in this silly business of you thinking that you can tell me what to wear or where to go or what to think!' Her temporary euphoric bubble was rapidly deflating. 'And I'm *not* about to start clubbing. I have too much on my plate at the moment,' she admitted with honesty, 'to even begin thinking about meeting a guy.'

'And I'm not prepared for that time to come,' Raoul said with grim determination. 'I don't want to be constrained to two evenings a week, and I don't want you telling me that this is about you. It's not. It's about Oliver, and you can't tell me that it's not better for a child to have both parents here.'

Sarah looked at him with dazed incomprehension. 'So…?'

'So you want nothing short of full time commitment? Well, you've got it. For Oliver's sake, I'm willing to marry you…'

CHAPTER SEVEN

FOR a few seconds Sarah wondered whether she had heard right, and then for a few more seconds she basked in the bliss of his proposal. Now that he had uttered those words she realised that this was exactly what she had wanted five years ago. His bags had been packed and she had been hanging on, waiting for him to seal their relationship with just this indication of true commitment. Of course back then his response had been to dump her.

'You're asking me to marry you,' she said flatly, and Raoul titled his head to one side.

'It makes sense.'

'Why now? Why does it make sense now?'

'I'm not sure what you're getting at, Sarah.'

'I'm guessing that the only reason you've asked me to marry you is because you don't like the thought of being displaced if someone else comes along.'

'Oliver's my son. Naturally I don't care for the thought of another man coming into your life and taking over my role.'

But would he have asked her to marry him if he hadn't happened to see her in a short skirt and a small top, making the most of what few assets she possessed, and jumped to all the wrong conclusions? He hadn't asked her to marry him when she had told him that she wanted the opportunity to meet someone with whom she could have a meaningful relationship, that there was more to life than sex...

Sarah reasoned that that was because, whatever she said, he had believed deep down that his hold over her was unbreakable. Historically, she had been his for the asking, and he knew that. Had he imagined that it was something she had never outgrown? Had he thought that underneath all her doubts and hesitation and brave denials she was really the same girl, eager and willing to do whatever he asked? Until it had been brought home to him, silly and mistaken though he was, that she might actually have *meant* what she said?

For Sarah, it all seemed to tie up. Raoul enjoyed being in control. When they had lived together on the compound all those years ago he had always been the one to take the lead, the one to whom everyone else instinctively turned when it came to decision making. Had the prospect of her slithering out of his reach and beyond his control prompted him into a marriage proposal?

'I didn't think that you ever wanted to get married,' she pointed out, and he gave an elegant shrug, turning to stare out of the window to where Oliver's appetite for the garden appeared to be boundless.

'I never thought about having children either,' he returned without hesitation, 'but there are you. The best-laid plans and so on.'

'Well, I'm sorry that Oliver's come along and messed up your life,' she said in a tight voice, and he spun round to look at her.

'Don't ever say that again!' His voice was low and sharp and lethally cold, and Sarah was immediately ashamed of her outburst because it hadn't been fair. 'I may not have planned on having children but I now have a child, and there is no way that I would wish it otherwise.'

'I'm sorry. I shouldn't have said that. But…look, it would be a disaster for us to get married.'

'I'm really not seeing the problem here. There's more than just the two of us involved in this…'

'So what's changed from when you first found out about Oliver?'

'I don't understand this. Are you playing hard to get because you think that I should have asked you to marry me as soon as I found out about Oliver?'

'No, of course not! And I'm not playing *hard to get*. I know that this isn't some kind of game. You don't *want* to marry me, Raoul. You just want to be in a position of making sure that I don't get involved with anyone else and jeopardise your contact and influence with Oliver, and the only way you can think of doing that is by putting a ring on my finger!'

She spun round on her heels and made for the door, but before she could reach it she felt his fingers on her arm and he whipped her back round to face him.

'You're not going to walk out on this conversation!'

'I don't want to carry on talking about this. It's upsetting me.'

Raoul shot her a look of pure disbelief. 'I can't believe I'm hearing this! I ask you to marry me and you're acting as though I've insulted you!'

'You want me to be grateful, Raoul, and I'm not. When I used to dream of being married it was never about getting a grudging proposal from a man who has an agenda and no way out!'

'This is ridiculous. You're blowing everything out of proportion. Oliver needs a family and we're good together.' But Raoul couldn't deny that the idea of her running around with other men had, at least in part, generated his urgent decision. Did that turn him into a control freak? No!

'In other words, all things taken into account, why not? Is that how it works for you, Raoul?' She couldn't bring herself to look at him. His hand was a band of rigid steel on her arm, even though he actually wasn't grasping her very hard at all.

Silence pooled around them until Sarah could feel herself beginning to perspire with tension. Why was it such a struggle to do what she knew was the right thing? Why was it so hard to keep her defences in place? Hadn't she learnt anything at all? Didn't she deserve more than to be someone's convenient wife, even though she happened to be in love with that *someone*? What sort of happy future could there be for two people welded together for the wrong reason?

'Look, I know that the ideal situation is for a child to have both parents at home, but it would be wrong for us to sacrifice our lives for Oliver's sake.'

'Why do you have to use such emotive language?' He released her to rake an impatient hand through his hair. 'I'm not looking at it as a *sacrifice*.'

'Well, how *are* you looking at it?'

'Haven't we got along for the past few weeks?' He answered her question with a question, which wasn't exactly an informative response.

'Yes, of course we have...' Too well, as far as Sarah was concerned. So well, in fact, that it had been dangerously easy to fall in love with him all over again—for which foolishness she was now paying a steep price. A marriage of convenience would have been much more acceptable were emotions not involved. Then she could have seen it as a business transaction which benefited all parties concerned.

'And I know you don't like hearing this particular truth,' Raoul continued bluntly, 'but we get along in other ways as well…'

'Why does it always come down to sex for you?' Sarah muttered, folding her arms. 'Is it because you think that's my weakness?'

'Isn't it?'

Suddenly he was suffocatingly close to her. Her nostrils flared as she breathed in his heady, masculine scent. Unable to look him in the face, she let her eyes drift to the only slightly less alarming aspect of his broad chest. The top two buttons of his shirt were undone, and she could glimpse the fine dark hair that shadowed his torso.

'There's nothing wrong with that,' Raoul murmured in a velvety voice that brought her out in goosebumps. 'In fact, I like it. So we get married, Oliver has a stable home life, and we get to enjoy each other. No more having to torture yourself with pointless Should we? Shouldn't we? questions…no more wringing of hands…no more big speeches about keeping our hands off one another while you carry on looking at me with those hot little eyes of yours…'

Although he hadn't laid a finger on her, Sarah felt as though he had—because her body was on fire just listening to the rise and fall of his seductive words.

'I don't look at you…that way…'

'You know you do. And it's mutual. Every time I leave you I head home for a cold shower.' He tilted her mutinous head so that she was looking up at him. 'Let's make this legal, Sarah…'

The sound of Oliver calling them from downstairs snapped Sarah out of her trance and she took a shaky step back.

'I can't drag you kicking and screaming down the aisle,' Raoul said softly as she turned to head down the stairs.

Sarah stilled and half looked over her shoulder. 'But think about what I've said and think about the consequences if you decide to say no.'

'Is there some sort of threat behind what you're saying, Raoul?'

'I have never used threats in my dealings with other people. I've never had to. Instead of rushing in and seeing everything insofar as it pertains to *you*, try looking at the bigger picture and seeing things insofar as they pertain to everyone else.'

'You're telling me that I'm selfish?'

'If the cap fits…'

'I'm just not as cynical as you, Raoul. That doesn't make me selfish.'

Raoul was stumped by this piece of incomprehensible feminine logic, and he shook his head in pure frustration. 'What's cynical about wanting what's best for our child? You need to think about my proposition, Sarah. Now, Oliver's getting restless, but just bear in mind that if *I* am not impressed by the thought of some guy moving in with you and taking over my role, how would *you* feel when some woman moves in with me and takes over *your* role…?'

Leaving her with that ringing in her head was the equivalent of a threat, as far as Sarah was concerned. Furthermore, for the rest of the day he treated her with a level of formality that set her at an uncomfortable distance, and she wondered whether this was his way of showing her, without having to spell it out, what life would be like should they go their separate ways, only meeting up for the sake of their child.

She resented the way he could so effectively narrow everything down in terms that were starkly black and white. Oliver needed both parents at home. They got along. There

was still that defiant tug of sexual chemistry there between
them. Solution? Get married. Because she had rejected
his original offer: *Become lovers until boredom sets in*.
Marriage, for Raoul, would sort out the thorny problem
of another man surfacing in her life, and also satisfy his
physical needs. It made such perfect sense to him that any
objection on her part could only be interpreted as selfish-
ness.

Ridiculous!

But, whether he had intended it that way or not, his point
was driven home over the next few days, during which he
came at appointed and prearranged times so that he could
take Oliver out. He had asked her advice and laughed when
she had told him that any restaurant with starched white
linen tablecloths and fussy waiters should be avoided at
all costs, but there was a patina of politeness he now ex-
uded which Sarah found horribly unnerving.

Of course she wondered whether she was imagining
it. His marriage proposal was still whirring around in her
head. Had that made her hyper-sensitive to nuances in his
demeanour?

She had tried twice to raise the topic, to explain her
point of view in a way that didn't end up making her feel
as if she was somehow *letting the side down*, but in both
instances his response had been to repeat that she had to
think it through very carefully.

'Wait and see how this arrangement works,' he had
urged her, 'before you decide to rush headlong into a decision that you might come to bitterly regret.'

In a few well-chosen words he had managed to sum her
up as reckless, irresponsible, and incapable of making the
right choices.

Again Sarah had tried to get a toe hold into an argument, but he had expertly fielded her off and she had been left stewing in her own annoyance.

And at the bottom of her mind crawled the uncomfortable scenario of Raoul finding someone else. Now that he had taken on board the concept of marrying someone, would it prove persuasive enough for him to actually consider a proper relationship? He had had a congenital aversion to tying himself up with someone else. His background had predicated against it. But then Oliver had come along and a chip in the fortress of his self-containment had been made. Then he had taken the step of asking her to marry him.

Of course for all the wrong reasons as far as she was concerned! But he *had* jumped an enormous hurdle, even if he *did* see it only as a logical step forward, all things considered.

What if, having jumped that hurdle, he now allowed himself to finally open up to the reality of actually taking someone else on board? What if he *fell in love*?

When Sarah thought about that, she found herself quailing in panic. *She* could give him long, moralising speeches about the importance of not getting married simply for the sake of a child. *She* could scoff at the idea of entering into a union as intimate as marriage without the right foundations in place, because she was scared that she would not be able to survive the closeness without wanting much, much more. But how thrilled would she be if he took himself off to some other woman and decided to tie the knot?

It could easily happen, couldn't it? Having a child would have altered everything for him, even if he barely recognised the fact. She wondered whether he had been changed enough to consider the advantages of having a permanent woman in his life—someone who could be a substitute mother. Sarah felt sick at the prospect of having a *step-*

mother in the mix, but on the subject of things *making sense* it certainly would make sense, down the road, for him to get married.

He would surely find it difficult to continue playing the field, always making sure that Oliver and whatever current woman of the day didn't overlap. Would he want to live the rest of his life like that? And what about when Oliver got older and became more alert to what was happening around him? Would Raoul want to risk having his private life judged by his own child? No, of course he wouldn't. If there was one thing she had learnt, it was that Raoul was capable of huge sacrifices when it came to Oliver. He would never countenance his own son seeing him as an irresponsible womaniser.

Sarah found herself frequently drifting off into such thoughts as they settled into their new house and began turning it into a home.

There was absolutely nothing to be done, décor-wise, because everything was of an exquisite standard, but the show home effect was quickly replaced with something altogether more cosy as family pictures were brought out of packing boxes and laid on the mantelpiece in the sitting room. The fridge became a repository for Oliver's artwork as she attached his drawings with colourful little magnets, and the woven throws her mother had given her when she had first moved to London turned the sofa in the conservatory into a lovely, inviting spot where she and Oliver could watch television. They went on short forays into the nearby village, locating all the essentials.

On the surface, everything was as it should be. It was only her endlessly churning mind that kept her awake at night and made her lose focus when she was in the middle of doing something.

Raoul continued to behave with grindingly perfect, gentlemanly behaviour, and Sarah found herself wondering on more than one occasion what he was getting up to on the evenings when he wasn't around.

She hadn't realised how accustomed she had become to seeing him pretty much every day, or at least being given some explanation of where he was and what he was doing on those days when he hadn't been able to make it. On the single occasion when she had tried fishing for a little information he had raised his eyebrows, tutted, and told her that really it wasn't any of her business, was it?

Two days before they were due to go to Devon to visit her parents Raoul returned Oliver to the house after their evening at a movie and, instead of leaving, informed her that the time had come to have a chat.

'I'll wait for you in the kitchen.' He had given her two weeks, and two weeks was plenty long enough. He wasn't used to hanging around waiting for someone else to make their mind up—especially when the matter in question should really have required next to no deliberation—but Raoul had taken a couple of steps back.

Although she was attracted to him, she had refused to become his mistress, and he didn't think that she had done so because she had been holding out for a bigger prize. The plain and simple truth was that she was no longer his number one adoring fan. He had hurt her deeply five years ago, and that combined with the hardship of being a single mother without much money to throw around had toughened her.

Raoul knew that there was no way he could push her into marrying him. He was forced to acknowledge that in this one area, he had no control. But biding his time had driven him round the bend—especially when he kept remembering how easy and straightforward things had been between them before.

She returned to the kitchen forty-five minutes later. She had changed into a pair of loose, faded jeans that sat well below her waist and a tee shirt that rode up, exposing her flat belly, when she stretched into one of the cupboards to get two mugs for coffee.

'So...' she said brightly, once they were both at the kitchen table with mugs of coffee in front of them. This kitchen, unlike the tiny one in the rented house, was big enough to contain a six-seater table. He sat at one end, and Sarah deliberately took the seat at the opposite end. 'You wanted to talk to me? I know I've said this a thousand times, but the house is perfect. I can't tell you what a difference it makes, and there's so much to do around here. I've already found a morning playgroup we can go to! It's just so leafy and quiet.'

Raoul watched her and listened in silence, waiting until she had rambled on for a while longer before coming to a halting stop.

'Two weeks ago I asked you a question.'

Having spent the entire two weeks thinking of nothing else *but* that question he had posed, Sarah now looked at him blankly—and received an impatient click of his tongue in response.

'I'm not going to hang around for ever waiting for you to give me an answer, Sarah. I've waited so that you have had time to settle into the house. You've settled. So tell me—what's the answer going to be?'

'I...I don't know...'

'Not good enough.' Raoul contained his mounting anger with difficulty.

'Can I have a few more days to think about it?' Sarah licked her lips nervously. 'Marriage is such a big step,' she muttered, by way of extra explanation.

'Likewise having a child.'

'Yes…but…'

'Are we going to go down the same monotonous route of self-sacrifice?'

'No!' Sarah cried, stung by his bored tone of voice.

'Then what's your answer to be?' He looked at her fraught face and thought that he might have been sentencing her to life in prison—and yet five years ago she would have exploded with joy at such a proposal. 'If you say no then I *walk away*, Sarah.'

'Walk away? What do you mean walk away? Are you saying that you're going to abandon Oliver if I don't agree to marry you?'

'Oh, for God's sake! When are you going to stop seeing me as a monster? I will never abandon my own flesh and blood!'

'I'm sorry. I know you wouldn't,' Sarah said, ashamed, because sudden panic had driven her to say the first stupid thing in her head. 'So what *are* you saying?'

'I'll find someone else,' Raoul told her bluntly, 'and we will get in touch with lawyers, who will draw up papers regarding settlement and visiting rights. You will see me only when essential, and only ever when it is to do with Oliver. Naturally I will have no control over who you see, don't see, or eventually become seriously involved with, and the same would apply to me. Am I spelling things out loud and clear for you?'

The colour had drained from Sarah's face. Presented with such a succinct action-and-consequence train of events, she felt her wildly scattered thoughts finally crystallise into one shocking truth. She would lose him for ever. He really would meet another woman and the question of love wouldn't even have to arise. He would regulate his love-life because he would have to, and she would be left on the outside…watching.

She wouldn't conveniently stop loving him just because he'd removed himself from her.

He might not love her, but he would be a brilliant father—and she would be spared the misery of *just not having him around*. Who had ever said that you could have it all?

She was sadly aware that she would settle for crumbs. She wanted to ask him what would happen when he got bored with her. Would he begin to conduct a discreet outside life? It was a question to which she didn't want an answer.

She had thought that any marriage without love would be doomed to failure. She had never imagined herself walking down the aisle knowing that the guy by her side was only there because he had found himself in the unenviable position of having no choice. Duty and responsibility were two wonderful things, but she hadn't ever seen them as sufficient. Raoul, on the other hand, had moved faster towards the inevitable—and she had to catch up now, because the stark alternative was even more unpalatable and she hated herself for her weakness.

'I'll marry you,' she agreed, daring to steal a look at his face.

Raoul smiled, and realised that he had been panicked at the thought that she might turn him down. He *never* panicked! Even when he had been confronted with a child he hadn't known existed, when he had realised that his life was about to be changed irrevocably for ever, he hadn't panicked. He had assessed the situation and dealt with it. But watching her, eyes half closed, he had been aware of a weird, suffocating feeling—as if he had stepped off the edge of a precipice in the hope that there would be a trampoline waiting underneath to break his fall.

He stood up, thinking it wise to cover the basics and

then leave—before she could revert to her previous stance, reconsider his offer and tell him that it was off, after all. She could be bewilderingly inconsistent.

'I'm thinking soon,' he said, feeling on a strange high. 'As soon as it can be arranged, to be perfectly honest. I'll start working on that straight away. Something small...' He paused to look at her pinkened cheeks. Her hair was tumbling over her shoulders and he wanted nothing more than to tangle his fingers into it and pull her towards him.

'Although you are the one who factored marriage into your dreams of the future,' he murmured drily, 'so it's up to you what sort of affair you want. You can have a thousand people and St Paul's Cathedral if you like...'

Sarah opened her mouth to tell him that anything would do, because it wouldn't really be a *true* marriage, would it? Yes, they had known each other once. Yes, they had been lovers, and she had been crazy enough to think that he had loved her as much as she had loved him, even if he had never said so. But he hadn't intended marrying her then, or even setting eyes on her again once he had left the country. He hadn't wanted her then and he didn't want her now, but marriage, for him, was the only way he could be a permanent and daily feature in his son's life. Because she had rejected the first offer on the table, which had been to be his mistress.

Approaching the whole concept of their union in the way he might a business arrangement, maybe he had thought that living together would be the lesser of two evils. They would have learned to compromise without the necessity of having to take that final, psychologically big step and commit to a bond sealed in the eyes of the law. Or maybe he had just thought that if what they had fizzled out it would just be a whole lot easier to part company if they had merely been living together. And by then

he would have had a much stronger foothold in the door—
might even have been able to fight for custody if he'd chosen to.

Racked with a hornets' nest of anxieties, she still knew
that it would be stupid to open up a debate on the worth
of a marriage that had yet to happen. What would that get
her? Certainly not the words she wanted to hear.

'Something small,' she said faintly.

'And traditional,' Raoul agreed. 'I expect you would
like that, and so would your parents. I remember you saying something about a bracelet that your grandmother had
given your mother, which she had kept to be passed on to
you when you got married? You laughed and said that it
wasn't exactly the most expensive trousseau in the world,
but that it meant a lot to both of you.'

'Isn't there *anything* that you've forgotten?' Sarah asked
in a tetchy voice. All her dreams and hopes were being
agonisingly brought back home to her on a painful tide of
self-pity. She thought that she might actually have been
hinting to him at the time when she had said that. 'Anyway,
I think she lost that bracelet.'

'She *lost* it?'

'Gardening. She took it off, to…er…dig, and it must
have got all mixed up with soil and leaves…' Sarah
shrugged in a suitably vague and rueful manner. 'So, no
bracelet to pass on,' she finished mournfully.

'That's a shame.'

'Isn't it?' She suddenly frowned. 'So…we get married
and live here…'

'In this house, yes.'

'And what will you do with your apartment?'

Raoul shrugged. His apartment no longer seemed to
have any appeal. The cool, modern soullessness of the
décor, the striking artwork that had been given the nod by

him but bought as an investment, the expensive and largely unused gadgets in the kitchen, the imposing plasma screen television in the den—all of it now seemed to belong to a person with whom he could no longer identify.

'I'll keep it, I expect. I don't need to sell it or rent it, after all.'

'Keep it for what?'

'What does it matter?'

'It doesn't. I was just curious.'

They were going to be married. It wouldn't be a marriage made in heaven, and Sarah knew that her own suspicious nature would torpedo any hope of it being successful. As soon as Raoul had told her that he would keep the apartment she had foreseen an unpalatable explanation. An empty apartment would be very handy should he ever decide to stray.

She tried her utmost to kill any further development on that train of thought. 'I suppose you have some sort of sentimental attachment to it?' she prompted.

Raoul shook his head. 'Absolutely none. Yes, it was the place I bought when I'd made my first few million, but believe it or not it's been irritating me lately. I think I've become accustomed to a little more chaos.' He grinned, very relaxed now that he could see a definite way forward and liked what he saw.

Suddenly the reality of Raoul actually *living* with them made her giddy with apprehension. Would there be parameters to their marriage? It wouldn't be a *normal* one, so of course there must be, but was this something she should talk about now? Were there things she should be getting straight before she entered into this binding contract?

'Er...we should really talk about...you know...'

He paused and looked down at her. She had one small hand resting on his arm.

'What your expectations are...' Sarah said stoutly.

Raoul's brows knitted into a frown. 'You want a list?'

'Obviously not *in writing*. That would be silly. But this isn't a simple situation...'

'It's as simple or as difficult as we choose to make it, Sarah.'

'I don't think it's as easy as that, Raoul. I'm just trying to be sensible and practical. I mean, for starters, I expect you'd like to draw up some kind of pre-nup document?' That had only just occurred to her on the spur of the moment—as had the notion that laying down guidelines might confer upon her some sort of protection, at least psychologically. The mind was capable of anything, and maybe—just maybe—she could train hers to operate on a less emotional level. At least to outward appearances. Besides, he would be mightily relieved. Although, looking at his veiled expression now, it was hard to tell.

'Is that what you want?' Raoul asked tonelessly—which had the instant effect of making Sarah feel truly horrible for having raised the subject in the first place.

In turn that made her angry, because why should *he* be the only one capable of viewing this marriage with impartial detachment? What was so wrong if she tried as well? He didn't know what her driving motivation for doing so was because he wasn't in love with her, but why should that matter? He didn't have the monopoly on good sense, which was his pithy reason for their marriage in the first place!

'It might be a good idea,' she told him, in the gentle voice of someone committed to being absolutely fair. 'We don't want to get in a muddle over finances later on down the road. And also...' She paused fractionally, giving him an opportunity for encouragement which failed to materialize. 'I think we should both acknowledge that the most we can strive for is a really good, solid friendship...'

Her heart constricted as she said that, but she knew that she needed to bury all signs of her love. On the one hand, if he knew how she really felt about him the equality of their relationship would be severely compromised. On the other—and this would be almost worse—he would pity her. He might even choose to remind her that at no point, *ever*, had he led her to believe that lust should be confused with something else.

It would be a sympathetic let-down, during which he might even produce a hankie, all the better to mop up her overflowing tears. She would never live down the humiliation. In short, she would become a guilty burden which he would consider himself condemned to bear for the rest of his life. Whereas if she feigned efficiency she could at least avert that potential disaster waiting in the wings.

That thought gave her sufficient impetus to maintain her brisk, cheery façade and battle on through his continuing unreadable silence.

'If you think that we're embarking on a sexless marriage...' Raoul growled, increasingly outraged by everything she said, and critical of her infuriating practicality—although he really shouldn't have been, considering it was a character trait he firmly believed in.

Sarah held up one hand to stop him in mid-flow. This would be her trump card—if it could be called such.

'That's not what I'm saying...' Released from at least *that* particular burden—of just not knowing what to do with this overpowering attraction she felt for him—Sarah felt a whoosh of light-headed relief race through her. 'We won't take the one big thing between us away...'

The hand on his arm softened into a caress, moved to rest against his hard chest, and she stepped closer into him, arching up to him, glad that she no longer had to try and fight the sizzling attraction between them.

Raoul caught her hand and held it as he stared down at her upturned face,

'So tell me,' he drawled softly, 'why didn't you just agree to be my lover? It amounts to the same thing now, doesn't it?'

'Except,' Sarah told him with heartfelt honesty, 'maybe I just didn't like the notion of being your mistress until I went past my sell-by date. Maybe that's something I've only just realised.' She hesitated. 'Do you…do you want to reconsider your proposal?'

'Oh, no…' Raoul told her with a slow, slashing smile, 'this is exactly what I want…'

CHAPTER EIGHT

A WEEK and a half later and Raoul wasn't sure that he had got quite what he had wanted—although he was hard pressed to put a finger on the reason *why*.

Sarah's histrionics were over. She no longer vacillated between wanting him and turning him away. She had stopped agonising about the rights and wrongs of their sleeping together.

In fact, on the surface, everything appeared to be going to plan. He had moved in precisely one week previously. For one day the house had been awash with a variety of people, doing everything it took to instal the fastest possible broadband connection and set up all the various technologies so that he could function from the cosy library, which had been converted into a study complete with desk, printer, television screens to monitor the stock markets around the world and two independent telephone lines. Through the window he could look out at the perfectly landscaped garden, with its twin apple trees at the bottom. It was a far more inspiring view than the one he had had from his apartment, and he discovered that he liked it.

The wedding would be taking place in a month's time.

'I don't really care when it happens,' Sarah had told him with a casual shrug, 'but Mum's set her heart on something more than a quick register affair, and I don't like to disappoint her.'

Thinking about it, that attitude seemed to character-ise the intangible change Raoul had uneasily noticed ever since she had accepted his marriage proposal.

True to her word, they were now lovers, and between the sheets everything was as it should be. Better. He touched her and she responded with fierce, uninhibited urgency. She was meltingly, erotically willing. With the lights turned off and the moonlight dipping into the room through a chink in the curtains they made love with the hunger of true sexual passion.

Just thinking about it was enough to make Raoul half close his eyes and stiffen at the remembered pleasure.

But outside the bedroom she was amicable but re-strained. He came through the front door by seven every evening, which was a considerable sacrifice for him, be-cause he was a man accustomed to working until at least eight-thirty most days. Yes, she asked him how his day had been. Yes, she would have cooked something, and sure she had a smile on her face as she watched him go outside with Oliver for a few minutes, push him on the swing, then return to play some suitably childish game until his son's bedtime beckoned. But it was almost as though she had manufactured an invisible screen around herself.

'Right. Have you got everything?' They were about to set off for Devon for their postponed visit to her parents. There was more luggage for this two-night stay than he would have taken for a three-week long-haul vacation. Favourite toys had had to be packed, including the over-sized remote controlled car which had been his first and much ignored present for Oliver, but which had risen up the popularity ladder as the weeks had gone by. Drinks had had to be packed, because four-year-olds, he'd been assured, had little concept of timing when it came to long car journeys. Several CDs of stories and sing-a-long nursery rhymes had been bought in advance, and Sarah had drily informed him that he had no choice when it came to listening to them.

She had made a checklist, and now she recited things from it with a little frown.

'Is it always this much of a production when you go to visit your parents?' he asked, when they were finally tucked into his Range Rover and heading away from the house.

'This is a walk in the park,' Sarah told him, staring out of the window and watching the outskirts of London fly past. 'In the past I've had to take the train, and you can't believe what a battle *that's* been with endless luggage and a small child in tow.' She looked round to make sure that Oliver was comfortable, and not fiddling with his car seat as he was wont to do, and then stared out of the window.

Weirdly, she always felt worse when they were trapped in the confines of a car together. Something about not having any escape route handy, she supposed. With no door through which she could conveniently exit, she was forced to confront her own weakness. Her only salvation was that she was trying very hard, and hopefully succeeding, to instil boundaries without having to lay it on with a trowel.

She was friendly with him, even though under the façade her heart felt squeezed by the distance she knew she had to create. She couldn't afford to throw herself heart and soul into what they had, because she knew that if she did she would quickly start believing that their marriage was real in every sense of the word—and then what protection would she have when the time came and his attention began to stray? He didn't love her, so there would be no buffer against his boredom when their antics in the bedroom ran out of steam.

Daily she told herself that it was therefore important to get a solid friendship in place, because that would be the glue to hold things together. But at the back of her mind she toyed with the thought that friendship might prove more than just glue. Maybe, just maybe, he would become reliant on a relationship forged on the bedrock of circumstance. He had proposed marriage as a solution, and how much more he would respect her if she treated it in the same calm, sensible, practical way he did.

She was determined to starve her obsession with him and get a grip on emotions that would freewheel crazily given half a chance.

The only time she really felt liberated was when they were making love. Then, when he couldn't see the expression on her face, she was free to look at him with all the love in her heart. Once she had woken up to go to the bathroom in the early hours of the morning, and she had taken the opportunity, on returning to bed, to stare. In sleep, the harsh, proud angles of his beautiful face were softened, and what she'd seen wasn't a person who had the power to damage, but just her husband, the father of her child. She could almost have pretended that everything was perfect...

As they edged out of London, heading towards Devon along the scenic route rather than the motorway, Oliver became increasingly excited at the sight of fields and cows and sheep, and then at his favourite game of counting cars according to their colour, in which her participation was demanded.

After an hour and a half his energy was spent, and he fell asleep with the abruptness of a child, still clutching the glossy cardboard book which she had bought earlier in the week to occupy him on the journey down.

'I expect you're a bit nervous about meeting my parents...' Sarah reluctantly embarked on conversation rather than deal with the silence, even though Raoul seemed perfectly content.

Raoul gritted his teeth at the ever-bland tone of voice which she had taken to using when the two of them conversed.

'Should I be?'

'I would be if I were in your shoes.' Sarah's eyes slid over to absorb the hard, perfect lines of his profile, and then she found it was a task to drag them away.

'And that would be because...?'

'I'm not sure what they'll be expecting,' she told him honestly. 'I haven't exactly blown your trumpet in the past. In fact when I found out that I was pregnant... Well, put it this way: wherever in world you might have been, you ears would have been burning.'

'I'm sure that will be history now that I'm around and taking responsibility for the situation.'

'But they'll still remember all the things I said about you, Raoul. I could have held everything back, but finding out that I was pregnant was the last straw. I was hormonal, emotional, and a complete mess. I got a lot off my chest, and I doubt my mother, particularly, will have forgotten all of it.'

'Then I'll have to take my chances. But thank you for being concerned on my behalf. I'm touched.' His mouth curved into a sardonic smile. 'I didn't think you had it in you.'

'There's no need to be sarcastic,' Sarah said uncomfortably.

'No? Well, I hadn't intended on having this conversation, but seeing that you're up for a bit of honesty... I go to bed with a hot-blooded, giving, generous lover, and wake up every morning with a stranger. You'll have to excuse me for my assumption that you wouldn't be unduly bothered one way or another what your parents' reaction to me is.'

Hot-blooded, giving, generous... If only he knew that those words applied to her in bed and out of it, by night and by day.

'I hardly think that you can call me a *stranger*,' Sarah protested on a high, shaky laugh. 'Strangers don't... don't...'

'Make love for hours? Touch each other everywhere? Experiment in ways that would make most people blush? No need to worry, Sarah. We're not exactly shouting, and Oliver's fast asleep. I can see him in my rearview mirror.'

Sarah could feel her cheeks burning from his deliberately evocative language.

What do you want? she wanted to yell at him. Did he want her to be the adoring, subservient wife-in-waiting, so that he could lap up her adulation safe in the knowledge that she had been well and truly trapped? When he certainly didn't adore *her*?

'Well, aren't you pleased that you were right?' she said gruffly. 'I can't deny that I find you very attractive. I always have.'

'Call me crazy, but I can smell a *but* advancing on the horizon...'

'There *is* no but,' Sarah told him, thinking on her feet. 'And I really don't know what you mean when you accuse me of being a stranger. Don't we share all our dinners together now that we're living under the same roof?'

'Yes, and your increasing confidence in the kitchen continues to astound me. What I'm less enthusiastic about is the Stepford Wife-to-be routine. You say the right things, you smile when you're supposed to, and you dutifully ask me interested questions about my working day... What's happened to the outspoken, dramatic woman who existed two weeks ago?'

'Look, as you said yourself, what we're doing is the right thing and the sensible thing. I've agreed to marry you and I don't see the point in my carrying on arguing with you...'

'I'm a firm believer that sometimes it's healthy to argue.'

'I'm tired of arguing, and it doesn't get anyone anywhere. Besides, there's nothing to argue about. You haven't let us down once. I'm surprised no one's sent men in white coats to take you away because they think you've lost the plot—leaving work so early every evening and getting in so late every morning.'

'I'd call it adjusting my body clock to match the rest of the working population.'

'And how long is *that* going to last?' She heard herself snipe with dismay, but there was no reaction from him.

After a while, he said quietly, 'If I had a crystal ball, I would be able to tell you that.'

Sarah bit down on the tears she could feel welling up. There was a lot to be said for honesty, but since when was honesty *always* the best policy?

'Maybe I'm leaving work earlier than I ever have because I have something to leave for...'

Oliver. Paternal responsibility had finally succeeded in doing what no woman ever had or ever would. Sarah diplomatically shied away from dragging that thorny issue out into the open, because she knew that it would lead to one of those arguments which she was so intent on avoiding. Instead she remained tactfully silent for a couple of minutes.

'That's true,' she said noncommittally. 'I should tell

you, though, before we meet my mum and dad, that they'll probably guess the reasons behind our sudden decision to get married…'

'What have you told them?' Raoul asked sharply.

'Nothing…really.'

'And what does *nothing…really* mean, Sarah?'

'I may have mentioned that you and I are dealing with the situation like adults, and that we've both reached the conclusion that for Oliver's sake the best thing we can do is get married. I explained how important it was for you to have full rights to your son, and that you didn't care for the thought of someone else coming along and putting your nose out of joint…'

'That should fill them with undiluted joy,' Raoul said with biting sarcasm. 'Their one and only daughter, walking down the aisle to satisfy *my* selfish desire to have complete access to my son. If your mother hadn't lost that heirloom bracelet she'd been hoping to pass on to you she probably would have gone out into the garden, dug a hole and buried it just to save herself the hypocrisy of a gesture for a meaningless marriage.'

'It's not a *meaningless marriage*.'

Sarah knew she had overstepped the self-assertive line. It was one thing being friendly but distant. It was another to admit to him that she was spreading the word that their marriage was a sham. Not that she had. She hadn't had the heart to mention a word of it to her parents. As far as she knew they thought that her one true love had returned and the ring soon to be on her finger was proof enough of happy endings. They had conveniently forgotten the whole dumping saga.

Raoul didn't trust himself to speak.

An awkward silence thickened between them until

Sarah blurted out nervously, 'In fact, as marriages go, it makes more sense than most.'

More uncomfortable silence.

She subsided limply. 'I'm just saying that there's no need to pretend anything when we get to my parents.'

'I'm not following you.' Raoul's voice was curt, and for a brief moment Sarah was bitterly regretful that she had upset the apple cart—even if the apple cart *had* been a little wobbly to start with.

She was spared the need for an answer by the sound of little noises from the back seat as Oliver began to stir. He needed the toilet. Could they hurry? Their uncomfortable conversation was replaced by a hang-on-for-dear-life panic drive to find the nearest pub, so that they could avail themselves of the toilets and buy some refreshments by way of compensation.

Oliver, now fully revived after his nap, was ready to take up where he had left off—with the addition of one of the nursery rhyme tapes. He proceeded to kick his feet to the music in the back, protesting vehemently every time a move was made to replace it with something more soothing.

He was the perfect safeguard against any further foolhardy conversations, but as the fast car covered the distance, only getting trapped in traffic once along the way, Sarah replayed their conversation in her head over and over again.

She wondered whether she really *should* have warned her parents about the reality of the situation. She questioned why she had felt so invigorated when they had been arguing. She raged hopelessly against the horrible truth—which was that maintaining a friendly front was like drinking poison on a daily basis. She asked herself whether she had done the right thing in accepting his marriage proposal, and then berated herself for acknowledging that she had because she couldn't trust herself ever to be able to deal with the sight of him with another woman.

But what if he *did* stray from the straight and narrow? What if he found marriage too restrictive, even with Oliver there to keep his eyes firmly on the end purpose? She had attempted to give that very real possibility house room in her head, but however many times she tried to pretend to herself that she was civilised enough to handle it, she just couldn't bring herself to square up to the thought. Should she add a few more ground rules to something that was getting more and more unwieldy and complex by the second?

She nearly groaned aloud in frustration.

'I think I'm getting a headache,' she said tightly, running her fingers over her eyes.

Raoul flicked a glance in her direction. 'I sympathise. I'm finding that "The Wheels on the Bus" can have that effect when played at full volume repeatedly.'

Sarah relaxed enough to flash him a soft sideways smile. She was relieved that the atmosphere between them was normal once again. It was funny, but although her aim was to keep him at a distance the second she felt him really stepping away from her she panicked.

'We'll be there before the headache gets round to developing.'

Sure enough, twenty minutes later she began to recognise some of the towns they passed through. Oliver began a running commentary on various places of interest to him, including a sweet shop of the old-fashioned variety which they drove slowly past, and Sarah found herself pointing out her own landmarks—places she remembered from when she was a teenager.

Raoul listened and made appropriate noises. He was

only mildly interested in the passing scenery. Small villages in far-off rural places did very little for him. If anything they were an unwelcome reminder of how insular people could be in the country—growing up as one of the children from the foster home in a town not dissimilar to several they had already driven through had been a sure-fire case of being sentenced without benefit of a jury.

Mostly, though, Raoul was trying to remain sanguine after her revelation that she had already prejudiced her parents against him.

His temper was distinctly frayed at the seams by the time he pulled up in front of a pleasant detached house on the outskirts of a picturesque town—the sort of town that he imagined Sarah would have found as dull as dishwater the older she became.

'Don't expect anything fancy,' she warned him, as the car slowed to a halt on the gravelled drive.

'After the build-up you've given your parents, believe me—I'm not expecting anything at all.'

Sarah flinched at the icy coldness in his voice.

'I did you a favour,' she whispered defensively, because she could think of no way of extricating herself from her lie. 'It saves you having to pretend.'

'There are times,' Raoul said, before launching himself out of the car, 'when I really wonder what the hell makes you tick, Sarah.'

He moved round to the boot, extracting their various cases, and slammed it shut—hard—just as Oliver, released from the restrictions of his car seat, flew up the drive towards the middle-aged couple now standing on their doorstep to throw himself at them. Sarah was following Oliver, arms wide open to receive their hugs.

Raoul took it all in through narrowed eyes as he began walking towards the house. Her father was stocky, his hair thinning, and her mother was an older version of Sarah, with the same flyaway hair caught in a loose bun, tendrils escaping all over the place just as her daughter's did, and wearing a long flowered skirt and a short-sleeved top with a thin pink cardigan. She was as slender as her husband was rotund, and she had Sarah's smile. Ready, warm, appealing.

So, he thought grimly, these were the people she had decided to disabuse. Two loving parents who had probably spent their entire lives waiting for the day their much loved only daughter would get married, settle down...only to hear that the getting married and settling down wasn't quite the kind they had had in mind.

Making his mind up, he walked towards them. The smile on his face betrayed nothing of what was going through his head.

'So nice to meet you...' He slung his arm over Sarah's shoulder and pulled her against him, feeling the tension in her body like a tangible electric current. Very deliberately, he moved his hand to caress the back of her neck under the tumble of fair hair. 'Sarah's told me so much about you both...' He looked down at her and pressed his thumb against the side of her neck, obliging her to look up at him. Her big green eyes were wary. 'Haven't you, sweetheart...?'

What was he playing at? Whatever it was, he was managing to blow a hole in her composure.

The gestures of affection hadn't stopped at the front door.

Yes, there had been moments of reprieve during the course of the afternoon, when Oliver had demanded attention and when she'd gone into the kitchen to help prepare the dinner with her mother, but the rest of the time...

On the sofa he was there next to her, his arm along the back, his fingers idly brushing her neck, while he played the perfect son-in-law-to-be by engaging her parents in all aspects of conversation which he knew would interest them.

She realised how much she had confided in him about her background, because now every scrap of received information had come home to roost. He quizzed them about her childhood. He produced anecdotes about things he remembered having been told like a magician pulling rabbits from a hat. He recalled something she had said in passing about her father always wanting to do something with bees, and much of their time, as they sat at the dinner table, was taken up with a discussion on the pros and cons of bee-keeping, about which he seemed to be indecently well informed.

Even if she *had* told her parents the truth about their relationship they would have been hard pressed to believe her based on Raoul's performance.

He engaged them on every level, and when she showed signs of taking a back seat he made sure to drag her right back into the conversation—usually by beginning his remark pointedly with the words, 'Do you remember, darling…?'

Every reminder brought back a fuzzy familiarity that further undermined her composure. He talked at length about the compound in Africa, and revealed what she had known from that random communication she had glimpsed ages ago—that he contributed a great deal to the compound. He listed all the improvements that had been made over time, and confided that he had actually employed someone to oversee the funding.

'Those were some of the most carefree months in my

entire life,' he admitted, and she knew that he was telling the absolute truth.

The complex, three-dimensional, utterly wonderful man she had fallen deeply in love with was well and truly out of the box in which she had tried, vainly, to shove him. Holding back the effect he had on her was like trying to shore up a dam with a toothpick.

The bedroom in which they had been put—her old bedroom newly revamped, but with all the mementoes of childhood still in evidence—did nothing to repair her frayed nerves.

She was as jumpy as a cat on a hot tin roof when, at a little after ten, they were shuffled off upstairs—because surely they must be exhausted after that long drive from London?

'And don't even *think* about getting up for Oliver,' her mother carolled as Sarah was leaving the kitchen. 'Your dad and I want to spend some time with him, so you just have yourselves a well-deserved lie-in! Lots planned for the weekend!'

Sarah crept upstairs to find Raoul already showered and waiting for her on the bed, where he was sprawled, hands folded under his head, wearing nothing but for a pair of dark boxer shorts. Instantly all thought left her head. Her body reacted the way it always did: liquefying and melting, and already anticipating the feel of his fingers on it.

But her emotions were all over the place, and she informed him that she was going to take a shower.

'I'll be waiting for you when you return,' Raoul told her, following her with his eyes as she disappeared into the adjoining shower room, which was small but perfectly adequate.

She reappeared twenty minutes later. He watched her

walk towards him, wearing nothing, and swiftly whipped the duvet over him—because a man could lose his mind at the sight of that glorious body, with its full, pouting breasts and smooth lines, and his mind was precisely what he needed at this very moment.

Sarah slid under the covers and turned towards him, covering his thigh with hers and splaying her fingers across his broad chest.

The shower had helped cool her down, but there was still a desperation in her as she slid further on top of him and felt the rock-hardness of his erection press against her. With a soft moan she parted her legs and moved sinuously against the shaft, her body aching and opening up for him. As the sensitised, swollen bud of her clitoris rasped against him she had to stop herself from groaning out loud.

Raoul shuddered, fighting the irresistible impulse to spin her onto her back and sate his frustration by driving into her.

'No,' he said unevenly.

Sarah wriggled on top of him. 'You don't mean that,' she breathed, panicked by that single word.

She dipped her head, covered his mouth with hers, felt him groan as he kissed her back. Hard. He flipped her onto her back and straddled her so that he could carry on kissing her.

Sarah arched away. Her breasts ached and tingled. She wanted the wetness of his mouth on her nipples, suckling them, driving her crazy. She desperately needed to feel his mouth licking and exploring between her legs, sending her to greater and greater heights until she needed him to thrust into her. She wanted the fragile balance she had forced onto their relationship restored, because without it she was all at sea, lost and struggling to find a foothold in stormy waters.

'*No*, Sarah! God!' Raoul sprang back from her, literally leapt off the bed and walked tensely towards the window, to stare outside until his body began to damn well do as it was told. 'Cover yourself up,' he told her harshly, because the distraction of her nudity was doing his head in.

Sarah squirmed until she was sitting up and drew her knees up, pulling the covers right the way to her chin while he continued to loom over her in the semi-darkness like a vengeful god.

She felt cheap and dirty, and the ramifications of how she had tackled her own wayward emotions slammed into her with the savagery of a clenched fist.

How could she ever have thought that she could separate herself? Peel away her emotions and leave intact the deep craving of her body to be satisfied under cover of darkness? She wasn't built like that. She was engulfed with a sudden sense of shame.

'This isn't working,' he told her with harsh condemnation.

'I don't know what you're talking about.'

'You know damn well what I'm talking about, Sarah!' He raked his fingers through his hair. He wanted to punch something.

'No, I don't! I thought today went really well! I mean, they like you…'

'Against all odds?' His mouth curled cynically.

'I didn't exactly *say* all those things I told you,' Sarah confessed in a small voice. 'I didn't really tell them about the state of our relationship. Of course they know how it ended between us five years ago, but I didn't tell them that we were only together now because of Oliver. I just couldn't face telling them the truth—at least not just yet…'

'Why are you only now coming clean on that score?'

'What difference does it make whether they know or

not? It's true, isn't it? One chance meeting,' she said bitterly, 'and both our lives changed for ever. What's that they say about the butterfly effect? Half an hour later and I would have finished cleaning that part of the office. Half an hour later and you would have left without even knowing that I was only metres away from you, in another part of the building...'

'I prefer not to dwell on pointless *what if?* scenarios.'

Sarah gazed down at her interlinked fingers. Raoul's reappearance in her life might have turned her world upside down, but for Oliver it had been nothing but the best possible outcome.

Her heart was beating so furiously inside her that she could scarcely breathe.

'That bracelet...'

Sarah looked up at him quickly, so aggressively dominant in the small bedroom. 'What about it?'

'Gold rope? With some kind of inscription on the outside? Your mother was wearing it. Looks like the gardening accident wasn't quite as terminal for the piece of jewellery as you imagined.'

'I...I... Maybe I was mistaken...'

'No,' Raoul told her coldly, 'maybe *I* was mistaken. I stupidly thought that you were willing to give this marriage a try, but you're not.'

His lack of anger was terrifying.

'I *am* giving it a try...'

'Really? Because you're sleeping with me?'

Sarah felt the slow boil of anger thread its way through her panic and confusion. Suddenly he was dismissive of the fact that they were sleeping together? What a noble guy! Anyone would have thought that making love was way down on his agenda, when it was the *only* thing he had placed any value on! The only thing he had *ever* placed any value on. How dared he stand there, like a headmaster in front of a disappointing and rebellious student, and preach to her that he wasn't satisfied?

'Weren't *you* the one who made such a great big deal about our *mutual attraction*? Our *sexual chemistry*?' she flung at him. 'Didn't you tell me that we had *unfinished business* and the only way we could possibly sort that out was by *jumping into bed together*? You have a very convenient memory when it comes to things you don't want to remember, Raoul!'

'Am I to be forever punished for being honest when we first reconnected, Sarah?'

'And am *I* to be punished for being honest now?' she returned just as quickly. '*You* made it clear what this marriage was going to be all about, didn't you?'

She hated the shard of hope inside her that still wanted to give him the chance to say something—to tell her that she was wrong, that it wasn't just about the fact that they had a child together.

His silence shattered her.

'I'm playing by *your* rules, Raoul, and I'm finding that they suit me just fine! In fact, I think you were right all along! Having sex and lots of it is really working wonders at getting you out of my system!'

She sensed his stillness and wanted to snatch the words back. But they were out in the open now, and she didn't know what to do with his continuing lack of response. She tried to recapture some of her anger but it was disappearing fast, leaving in its wake regret and dismay.

'So the sex is all that matters to you, I take it?'

'Yes, of—of course it is…' she stammered, bewildered by that remark. 'Just like it is to you. And responsibility too, of course… We're doing this for Oliver, because it's always better for a child to have both parents at home. We're being sensible...practical...'

'What story are you going to spin your mother when it comes to the heirloom bracelet?'

'Wha...?'

'I one hundred percent agree with you. Heirlooms to be handed over are for brides who actually *want* to be married.'

'You're not being fair, Raoul.'

'I'm being perfectly fair. I had actually thought we had more going for us than just physical attraction, but I was wrong.' He began walking towards the door.

Sarah watched him, frantically trying to process what he had said.

His voice was flat and composed and as cold as ice. 'I've got your message loud and clear, Sarah. It's always good to have the rules laid bare...'

CHAPTER NINE

SARAH lay frozen for a few minutes. Now that she wanted to recall everything he had said, so that she could sift through his words and get them to make sense, she found that her thoughts were in a jumble. Her heart was beating so furiously that she could scarcely catch her breath, and she had broken out in a film of perspiration. Her nakedness was a cruel reminder of how she had attempted to drown her misery in making love.

She could get herself worked up at the thought of Raoul using *her*, but only now was she appreciating that she had been equally guilty of using *him*—even if she had tried to tell herself that that couldn't possibly be the case, because wasn't sex all he had wanted from her from the very start?

Where had he gone?

His self-control was such a part and parcel of his personality that to see him stripped of it had shaken her to her core.

Or had she been mistaken? Was he just angry with her?

With a little cry of horror and shaky panic, Sarah flung the covers off her and scrambled around the room to fling on a pair of jogging bottoms and an old long-sleeved jumper—a left-over reminder of her teenage years, when she had been in the school hockey team.

The house was dark and quiet as she tiptoed into the

hall. Her parents had never been ones to burn the midnight oil, and they would be fast asleep in their bedroom at the far end of the corridor. Oliver's door was ajar, and she peeped in, through habit, to see him spread flat on the bed, having kicked off his quilt, a perfect X-shape, lightly snoring.

Just in case, though, she made sure not to turn on the lights, and so had to grope her way down the stairs until her eyes adjusted to the darkness and she could move more quickly, checking first the kitchen, then the sitting room.

It wasn't a big house, so there was a limited number of rooms she could check, and her anxiety increased with each empty room. After twenty minutes, she acknowledged that Raoul just wasn't in the house.

The temperature had dropped, and she hugged herself as she quietly let herself outside.

At least his car was still there. She hurried down to the road and glanced in both directions. Then, as she headed back towards the house, a faint noise caught her ears and she stealthily made her way to the back of the house.

The garden wasn't huge, but it backed onto fields so there was an illusion of size. To one side was her mother's vegetable plot, and towards the back, through a wooden archway that had been planted with creeping wisteria, was a gazebo. Her father's potting shed was right at the very bottom of the garden. Trees and shrubbery formed a thick perimeter.

Walking tentatively through the archway, she spotted Raoul immediately. He was in the gazebo, sitting with his head in his hands. She paused, and then walked quietly towards him, feeling him stiffen as she got nearer although he didn't look up at her.

'I'm really sorry,' she said helplessly.

Just when she thought that he wasn't going to reply at all, he looked up and shrugged his broad shoulders.

'What for? You were being honest.'

'I was just trying to be mature about the whole thing...'

Raoul flung his head back and stared up, away from her, and in the fierce, proud, stubborn set of his features she could see the little boy who'd grown up in a foster home, learning young how to hide himself away and build a fortress around his emotions.

She rested her hand on his forearm and felt him flinch, but he didn't pull it away and for some reason that seemed like a good sign.

'I gave you what you wanted,' Raoul said, his eyes still averted. 'At least I gave you what I thought you wanted. Don't you like the house?'

'I love it. You know I do. I've told you so a million times.'

'I've never done that before, you know. I've never let myself be personal when it comes to choosing things for another person, but I made it personal this time.'

'I know. You wanted Oliver to have the very best.'

'I very much doubt whether Oliver cares that there's a bottle-green Aga in the kitchen or not.'

Her heart skipped a beat. 'What are you trying to say?'

'Trying? I thought it had been obvious all along.' He glanced across at her and her breath caught painfully in her throat. 'I wanted you to marry me. Maybe at the beginning I didn't think it was necessary. Maybe at the beginning I was still clinging to the notion that I was a free, independent guy who happened to have found himself with a child. It took me a while to realise that the freedom I'd spent my life acquiring wasn't the kind of freedom I wanted after all.'

'I don't want to tie you down,' Sarah said quietly. 'I did.

Once. When we were out there. I thought you were just the most wonderful thing that had ever happened to me in my entire life. I built all sorts of castles in the air, and then when you dumped me my whole world fell to pieces.'

'I did what I thought was right at the time.'

'And I understand that now.'

'Do you? Really? I look at the way you are with your family, Sarah, and I see how badly you must have been affected by our break-up. You've grown up with security and a sense of your own place in the world. I grew up without either. I never allowed myself to get too close to anyone, and even when we met again, even after I found out that I was a father, I kept holding on to that. It was different with Oliver. Oliver is my own flesh and blood. But I still kept holding on to the belief that I wasn't to let anyone else in.'

'I know. Why do you think it's been so hard for me, Raoul? You've no idea what it's been like, standing on the side, wondering if the time will ever come when I can just get inside that wall you've spent a lifetime building around yourself.' She sighed and dragged her eyes away from him. The moon was almost full and it was a cloudless night. 'Look, you're not the only one who was afraid of getting hurt.'

Raoul opened his mouth to protest that he wasn't scared of anything, and then closed it.

'I know you hate the thought of anyone being able to hurt you.'

'God, it's ridiculous how well you seem to know me.'

There was wry, accepting amusement in his voice and, heartened by that, Sarah carried on.

'I spent so many years thinking of you as the guy who broke my heart that when we met again I *still* wanted to think of you as the guy who broke my heart. Yes, there was Oliver, and there was never any question that I would tell you about him and accept the consequences, but it was so important for me to keep you at a distance. And you kept looking at me and reminding me how much I still wanted you.'

'And yet you could never come right out and say it,' Raoul inserted gruffly. 'You were driving me crazy. I wanted to sleep with you and I knew you wanted to sleep with me, and you carried on fighting it. Every time I looked at you it was as though we had never been separated by five years. I didn't even know it at the time, but I let you into my life five years ago, Sarah, and you shut the door behind you and never left. I only thought you did.' He groped for her hand and linked her fingers through his. 'Asking you to marry me was a very big deal for me, Sarah.'

'You said that we were unfinished business...'

'If that's all you were to me I would never have asked you to marry me, because it wouldn't have bothered me if eventually you found another man.'

'You were worried about losing Oliver.'

'I think I knew, deep down, that that wouldn't happen. You would have allowed me all the access I wanted—and, let's face it, it's not as though children of parents who don't live together end up forgetting who the absent parent is. No, I asked you to marry me because I wanted you in my life and I couldn't envisage life without you in it.'

'Oh, Raoul.' Tears gathered in the corners of her eyes and she smiled at him, a smile of pure joy.

'I love you, Sarah. That's why I asked you to marry me. Like a fool, I'm only now admitting it to myself. I loved you five years ago and I never stopped. I love you and want you and need you, and when you retreated into that shell of yours and only came out at night when we were making love, it was as though the bottom of my world had dropped out.'

Sarah flung her arms around him, almost sending them both toppling off the narrow seat, and buried her head in the crook of neck.

'Are you telling me that you love me too?'

She heard the broken quality of his voice and knew that underneath the self-assurance there was still uncertainty—a legacy that he hadn't yet left behind.

'Of *course* I love you, Raoul!' She kissed his cheeks, his eyes, and her hands fluttered across his harshly beautiful face until he captured them and kissed the tips of each of her fingers. 'I was so scared of getting hurt all over again,' she admitted, with a catch in her voice. 'I thought I'd be able to handle our relationship, *us*, without getting involved. I mean, I was so shocked when I saw you again. But I told myself that I'd grown up and learnt lessons from the way things had turned out between us. I told myself that I was free of whatever influence you had over me...'

She thought back to those many weeks when he had infiltrated her life and shown her flimsy notions up for the nonsense they had been from the very beginning.

She lay back against him and stared up at the bright constellations. 'When Oliver met you and the two of you didn't...um...'

'Exactly hit it off?' It seemed like a very distant memory now.

'Yes... Well, I realised that the two of you would have to learn to interact, and I knew that the only way that would happen would be if I intervened. I just didn't take into account how devastating it would be to have you back in my life, virtually full-time... We were both older...somehow it felt like I'd started seeing the real you...and I fell in love with you all over again.'

'Was that why you broke my heart by pushing me away?'

'Stop teasing. I didn't really break your heart…'

'You did. Into a thousand pieces. I came here intending to give you everything. I wasn't going to let you get away with being my woman by night and a person I barely recognised by day.'

'And you thought I'd rejected you…'

'Somehow just wanting me for my body didn't work.' He laughed with incredulity. 'I can't believe I've just said that.'

'Of course,' Sarah breathed, in a lingering, seductive voice, 'wanting you for your body isn't *such* a terrible thing…especially now that you know that I want you for so much more…'

They were married a month later, at the little village church. It was a quiet affair, with friends and family mingling easily and getting to know one another, and Sarah had never felt happier than when Raoul slipped that ring on her finger and whispered how much he loved her.

And then her parents had Oliver for ten days while they had a blissful honeymoon in Kenya. For their last three days they went back to the compound in Mozambique where they had first met, so that they could both see the changes that had taken place over the five years. And there were many changes, thanks to Raoul's generous contributions over the years, although the house with all the steps, which they had shared along with the other gap year students, was still there, and a moving reminder of where it had all begun.

Even the log was still there—the very same log she had sat on, filled with misery and despair. It had survived the punishing weather, and she wondered who else had sat on it and thought about their loved ones.

The new batch of students working there seemed so young that it made her laugh.

They finally returned to London, and the very first thing Raoul said, on walking through the front door, was that they needed a house in the country.

'I never thought I'd step outside London again,' he confessed as they lay in bed on their first night back. 'But I'm beginning to think that there's something quite appealing about all that open space...'

He gently smoothed her hair back from her face, and she smiled at him with such tenderness and love that he felt, once again, that feeling of safety and a sense of completion.

'We could go there on weekends...somewhere in Devon...it's not that far...'

'Yes,' Sarah replied seriously, 'that might not be a bad idea. I mean, it would be great to see more of Mum and Dad—especially now that you've managed to convince Dad that he should take up the bee-keeping thing, with lots of help from you—and the children would like it...'

'Already planning an extension to our family?' Raoul laughed softly, and slipped his hand underneath her lacy top.

They had made love less than an hour ago, but just the feel of her swollen nipple between his fingers was sufficient to rouse him to an instant erection. He pushed the top up, licked the valley between her breasts, which was still salty and damp with perspiration, and settled himself to suckle on the sweet pink crests.

'I thought we were talking,' Sarah laughed.

'Fire away. I'm all ears.'

'I can't talk...when...' She gave up, arching her body to greet his eager mouth as he sucked and teased her breasts, then moved lower down to torment the little bud already swollen in anticipation.

The flicking of his tongue stifled all hope of conversation, and it was a long time before she whispered drowsily, 'Not so much *planning* an extension to our family as thinking there might be one arriving in the next few months or so…'

Raoul propped himself up and looked at her with urgent interest.

'You're pregnant?'

'I was going to tell you as soon as I did a test—but, yes, I think I am. I recognise all the signs…'

And she *was* pregnant.

She had almost stopped believing in fairytales, but now she had to revise that opinion—because whoever said that fairytales *didn't* come true…?

* * * * *

A sneaky peek at next month...

MODERN™

INTERNATIONAL AFFAIRS, SEDUCTION & PASSION GUARANTEED

My wish list for next month's titles...

In stores from 20th January 2012:

☐ An Offer She Can't Refuse – Emma Darcy
☐ A Night of Living Dangerously – Jennie Lucas
☐ Marriage Behind the Façade – Lynn Raye Harris
☐ Back in the Lion's Den – Elizabeth Power

In stores from 3rd February 2012:

☐ An Indecent Proposition – Carol Marinelli
☐ A Devilishly Dark Deal – Maggie Cox
☐ Forbidden to His Touch – Natasha Tate
☐ Running From the Storm – Lee Wilkinson
☐ The Shameless Life of Ruiz Acosta – Susan Stephens

Available at WHSmith, Tesco, Asda, Eason, Amazon and Apple

Just can't wait?

MILLS & BOON
BOOK CLUB

2 Free Books!

Join the Mills & Boon Book Club

Want to read more **Modern**™ books? We're offering you **2 more** absolutely **FREE!**

We'll also treat you to these fabulous extras:

- **Books up to 2 months ahead of shops**
- **FREE home delivery**
- **Bonus books with our special rewards scheme**
- **Exclusive offers and much more!**

Get your free books now!

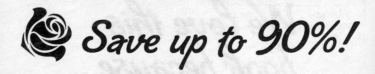

Special Offers

Every month we put together collections and longer reads written by your favourite authors.

Here are some of next month's highlights— and don't miss our fabulous discount online!

On sale 20th January

On sale 20th January

On sale 3rd February

On sale 3rd February

Save 20% on all Special Releases